THE ROSEBUD GIRLS

A ROSEBUD NOVEL

JULIA CLEMENS

D1495368

PICKLED PLUM PUBLISHING

To all my girls. My very first best friends, my sisters.

CHAPTER ONE

"EXCUSE ME, Ma'am, but you can't go back there," an extremely attractive waiter said to Callie as she rushed past him and on toward her destination. He would have been even more good-looking had he not just called her *Ma'am*.

"Ma'am," the waiter called again as she ignored his directive. Callie hadn't gotten to the place she was in her life by giving in when a beautiful man asked her to do something for him.

"Saffron Pierce!" Callie called out as soon as she entered the bustling kitchen her best friend not only directed but owned. Well, she owned a third of it. Callie began to examine the silver space for the woman she was searching for. Gleaming counters stood to her right, covered with bowls and cutting boards piled with delectable-looking ingredients, but no Saffron. Shiny, stainless-steel walk-in refrigerators and matching top-of-the-line stovetops lined up on her left, but still no Saff.

"I'm sure Chef will be happy to oblige you if you'd just wait a moment at the bar." The cute waiter was becoming annoying.

"You and I both know that Saffron is much too busy to come out to the bar to talk to anyone, even her best friend," Callie snapped at the waiter, who took a step back at the words *best friend*.

Knowing she had sufficiently scared the boy off, Callie was about to continue with her plan. She was always a woman with a plan, but she began to feel sorry for the man she'd just turned her back on. He was only doing his job, after all.

"I'll be sure to let Saffron know you had nothing to do with my interruption of her work. In fact, I'll tell her you did everything beside bodily hold me down in order to keep her kitchen free of riffraff like me," Callie added and even punctuated her words with a smile.

"I would never presume you were riffraff," the waiter said and then noticed Callie's smile and visibly relaxed, seeming to understand that she was teasing him. He drew in a deep breath. "Thank you," he said and hurried back out of the kitchen and away from his employer. Callie knew that Saffron ran a tight operation, but she'd had no idea her best friend had her employees living in fear of her. Or maybe the guy was afraid of Callie.

Her smile returned at that thought. Callie thought it was healthy to instill a bit of fear in people, especially beautiful people like the waiter. Life shouldn't be too easy for anyone. It hadn't been on her.

"Saffron," Callie called out, forgetting about the waiter and walking further into the kitchen.

Several people working around her looked up but none had the hot-cocoa-colored eyes of her best friend.

Callie was about to gather them around and demand the whereabouts of her friend when she heard a bored voice ask, "What do you want, Callie?"

Callie glanced behind her and saw Saffron stirring a pot of something that had to be delicious—everything Saffron made was delicious. Saffron put down her spoon and made her way around to Callie's side, coming to stand next to a man who was frying fish in three different pans.

"Alex, less salt, more butter," she said with narrowed eyes. "If I have to tell you again, this job will no longer be your concern."

Alex gulped before nodding at the formidable woman before him. Granted, Saffron was all of five foot three, but with her arms crossed over her chest like that, most people wouldn't mess with her.

Callie wasn't most people.

"Again, Callie, what do you want? If you can't tell, I'm a little busy here," Saffron said as she waved her hand, indicating the entire kitchen. If Callie knew Saffron, her friend was involved in each and every dish that was being created in that kitchen.

Sure enough, Saffron moved again, this time to the prep area where a young woman stood chopping vegetables. Callie followed.

"Thinner than that, Suzie," Saffron said as she examined the onions the young woman was chopping.

"You weren't answering my texts," Callie said, responding to her friend's previous question. Callie had known bugging Saffron at work wasn't the way to win her over, but she was becoming desperate. They were on a timeline, and if she didn't get Saffron on board that day, they might lose the thing they'd wanted ever since the two women were eighteen. It was a long time ago, too many years ago for Callie to actually admit, but it was still important to her. She had to believe it was just as important to Saffron as well.

"I replied last night," Saffron pulled her phone out of her pocket and then showed the screen to her friend where she had indeed answered one text.

I'm alive, the short text said in response to Callie's four texts before that, which had ended with *Are you even alive?*

But Saffron knew very well that wasn't the text Callie was referring to.

"The lodge, Saff," Callie said as her best friend tried to move to another part of the kitchen once again, but Callie put out an arm to stop her.

"I read the group text," Saffron said and then pursed her lips. It was never good when Saff pursed her lips.

"But you didn't respond," Callie said, not allowing herself to be dissuaded. She would never have made it as Saff's best friend if she'd been scared off every time Saff pursed her lips.

"I just...no one has responded," Saffron said, and Callie couldn't deny that.

Callie, Saffron, Kenzie, Hazel, and Laurel had been just eighteen when they decided they would one day own the Rosebud Lodge. Some might say it was a cute dream of teenaged girls, but there was more to what they'd promised than that. The lodge was a part of Rosebud history, and although many of them had moved on from their small town in Northern California some years before, Callie knew that the lodge would bring them all home. More importantly, back to one another. They'd lived distanced lives for long enough. It was time for home.

"I'm not here to talk about anyone else, Saff," Callie said, and Saffron shook her head as she looked around at her kitchen that seemed to have paused, everyone watching what was happening between their head chef and Callie.

Saffron took her friend by her arm, leading her back to her office and barking over her shoulder, "Back to work."

Saffron had once confided in Callie that because she was a female chef, she felt the need to be harder and tougher than any male counterpart would be. Saffron was often the lone female in a very male-dominated industry and some people looked at her sex as a weakness. But she had climbed and clawed her way to the top, each day working harder than the one before.

The kitchen began bustling again before Saffron closed her office door behind Callie and herself.

"You see what it's like out there," Saffron said, crossing her arms as she leaned against the door behind her.

Callie nodded as she tucked her shoulder-length blonde hair behind her ears. It was practically a circus, and Saffron was the ringmaster.

"I don't have time for a shower most days. I only make the time because not taking one would be a health code violation," Saffron said, and Callie understood that. Her best friend worked way too many hours.

Thinking about all Saffron had missed out on because of her job troubled Callie. She sat down on the sofa that she knew her friend often made her bed on nights when she was just too exhausted to make the twenty-minute trek to her condo in the city.

"I know," Callie said again. She recognized Saffron's situation. But she also knew the kind of opportunity the lodge would be for them. For Saffron in particular.

The Rosebud Lodge had at one time been a premiere vacation location. Just north of San Francisco and west of the gorgeous Napa Valley, Rosebud Lodge had made a name for itself in the years before. Sitting between two extensive vineyards, and just a half an hour from some beautiful beaches, the location was prime for anyone looking for a relaxing vacation or even just a night away. But the lodge had declined some in recent years, the family who owned it not knowing what to do when word-of-mouth wasn't enough to keep it in the limelight. And so the family was now selling, and Callie had to jump at the chance. They all had to. The lodge wasn't just a pretty place in their hometown, it was a part of who she and her friends were. They just had to remember that. And Callie was going to make sure they did. Especially Saffron.

"Where are your partners?" Callie asked as she looked out the window that divided Saffron's office from her kitchen, already knowing full well where they were. Well, at least where they *weren't*. In that kitchen working their butts off like Saffron was.

Saffron muttered something under her breath that didn't sound very ladylike, and Callie fought the urge to smile. She was glad Saffron hadn't lost all of her fire when it came to her lazy partners. Sometimes, at least to Callie, it seemed like Saffron just accepted that her colleagues expected her to do all the work. She was glad that wasn't the case.

The agreement between Saffron and her two partners had been simple. They all put in the seed money for the brick-and-mortar restaurant they'd been dreaming about. They each came into their restaurant with relatively equal footing; they had all started Saffron in a prestigious San Francisco kitchen, although Saffron was a few years younger than the others, and had therefore graduated from culinary school a few years later. Because of that, the male associates had seemed wary about allowing Saffron in on their venture, at least in the beginning. But she had quickly proved her worth to the people Callie liked to call 'those idiot men' in her mind. When their agreement was drawn up, not only was the cost of the restaurant supposed to be equally split three ways, which it had been, the work was supposed to be split in thirds as well. And yet here Saffron ran around the kitchen alone, night after night, because her partners knew they could do this to her and get away with it. Saffron expected nothing short of perfection, and if her counterparts wouldn't be there in the evening to watch over their employees, they knew Saffron would. So she did. Every day.

And although Saffron did all the work, her partners were

always there to accept the praises. No one knew Saffron had done all of the heavy lifting on her own because the three chefs were equally hailed as culinary geniuses.

"When was the last time you had a day off?" Callie asked. Yes, she was needling her best friend, but she needed Saffron to see that her current situation wasn't all that great. And by 'not that great', she meant 'totally awful'. And definitely not as good as running her very own kitchen at the lodge would be.

Saffron once again muttered the word, and this time Callie raised her eyebrows. It wasn't like her friend to curse. If Saffron's mom had been anywhere in the vicinity, she would have started chasing her only daughter with a bar of soap to wash that mouth out. Mrs. Pierce had raised five children, four of them boys, and she didn't mess around when it came to the language she allowed the next Pierce generation to use.

"And I'm guessing you don't get more of the profits the way that you should, seeing as you are the only one here day in and day out," Callie said, nodding toward the stack of papers on Saffron's desk. She doubted there was an identical stack on either of Saffron's partners' desks.

"I get it, Cal. I see what you're trying to do. But this is my life. My entire livelihood. I wish the lodge had come on the market ten years ago when we were only considering buying this place. But now I'm in too deep. I can't just leave it all," Saffron said as her eyes drifted toward the kitchen. She stood and threw her office door open.

"That sauce is burning, Miguel!" Saffron shouted, and the entire room looked her way.

"I, uh," stammered a man who must be Miguel.

"If I can smell that from here, through a closed door, I know there is no way you could have missed it," Saffron continued to yell, and Miguel began to stir the pot in question.

"Don't try to save it. Throw it out. Start again," Saffron

demanded, and she waited impatiently for her commands to be followed before slamming the door to her office shut again.

"Do you love it?" Callie asked as her best friend still seethed.

"Do you know what would have happened if Miguel had served that sauce?" Saffron asked, pacing the length of the small office. "And he would have served it if I hadn't said anything."

Saffron paused, leaning heavily against the door. "It's not bad enough that a critic could show up in our dining room any evening of the week, but now with YouTube and food bloggers and Yelp, everyone is a critic. Ev-er-y-one," Saffron enunciated every syllable. "One bad review at just the right moment; it can take us down. Everything we've built."

Leaning against the door, Saffron began to slide down it and then seemed to realize what she was doing before standing up straight again.

"The food world is competitive in the city," Callie said before adding, "unlike in a small town like Rosebud."

Saffron narrowed her eyes.

"A bad review could kill the lodge too," Saffron stated.

"It could," Callie admitted. "But not quite the swift death blow that would be dealt here. People in the country are more forgiving. More inclined to give a second chance."

Callie knew Saffron couldn't disagree with that. So instead her friend pushed herself off of the door and stood in front of Callie.

"I have to get back out there," Saffron said, pointing toward her kitchen.

"You didn't answer my question," Callie said. She wasn't going to leave until Saffron agreed to go in on the lodge. Callie wouldn't be so adamant if Saffron adored her life in the city. But that clearly wasn't the case. Saffron had left Rosebud to prove herself. And she'd done that. Now it was time to come home. Use those delicious talents she'd learned in her own hometown.

"What question?" Saffron asked as she began tapping her toe and huffing her dark, curly bangs away from her face. The woman truly was very impatient.

"Do you love it?" Callie asked, pointing to the kitchen.

Saffron drew in a deep breath.

"I love cooking," Saffron said, and Callie nodded. She knew that.

"That's not what I asked, though. Do you love this? This job, this restaurant."

"It's my restaurant," Saffron stated, putting her hands on her chef-coat-covered hips.

"With two men you are beginning to hate. But, yes, it's your restaurant. However, you have yet to answer my question."

"I *am* starting to hate them," Saffron said quietly as if the thought hadn't occurred to her. Callie didn't doubt it. Her friend was too busy to actually think about anything other than keeping her kitchen in top shape.

"Do you love your job, Saff?" Callie asked. "Is that why you can't leave? Because you have nothing left here to prove. You built a restaurant from the ground up. And it is successful beyond belief. I saw the packed dining room. The four-week wait list. You have it all."

"And you're asking me to walk away from it," Saffron said as she met Callie's blue eyes.

"Not if you love it," Callie said. And she wouldn't. As much as she wanted the lodge and as much as she wouldn't continue forward without Saffron, she wanted her friend's happiness more. And if this restaurant gave that to her, Callie would never ask her to leave.

Saffron's gaze left Callie's as she scanned the kitchen. Callie saw pride fill her friend's eyes. But she saw something else. Exhaustion.

"You could sell your portion back to the guys," Callie said.

She knew the contract between Saffron and her partners well because she'd been there when it had been drafted by the three of them. Saffron had wanted her real-estate-mogul best friend at her side as she made the biggest career decision of her life. Although, the description *mogul* was only ever used by Saffron and her other friends, not herself. Callie was successful but had a ways to go before she'd deserve that word, she thought.

"I *could* walk away," Saffron said softly, giving her very first indication that Callie might be right.

"Don't you miss home?" Callie asked, and Saffron nodded immediately. She had taken to the big city, but it would never be her home, and Callie knew it as well as Saffron did.

"I'm tired," Saffron finally admitted, and Callie nodded. "I'm tired of doing all of the work, I'm tired of trying to stay on top, I'm tired of carrying the load of three people, I'm tired of working so hard for something I no longer love," Saffron said, her words becoming louder with each one she spoke.

Despite knowing that, Callie's heart broke for Saffron nonetheless. This restaurant had been her dream ever since she'd graduated from culinary school.

"I'm sorry," Callie whispered, and Saffron nodded as liquid filled her eyes. She quickly banished that with the back of her hand before it could turn into tears.

"I would run the kitchen on my own?" Saffron asked, and Callie nodded. Of course Saffron would. Although....

"I mean, the lodge has their own chef right now who we probably shouldn't fire, but you'd be the boss," Callie said.

Saffron crossed her arms. "I wouldn't have to run every decision by you and the girls?"

"Not when it comes to the kitchen. That would be your domain," Callie promised.

"I have to run everything by the guys here. I can't make a change to a single appetizer without both of them signing off on it, even though they haven't been to the kitchen in months," Saffron said, probably more to herself than to Callie.

"Why don't *you* just buy the lodge?" Saffron suddenly asked, and Callie immediately met Saffron's intense gaze.

They both knew Callie had the capital—and then some—to buy the lodge outright on her own. And she had the business know-how to run the lodge herself. What she couldn't humanly do, she could hire out, and her friends had always said Callie had the Midas touch when it came to anything real estate.

"Because I want all of you girls by my side..." Callie thought about leaving it there, but she couldn't. She had to tell Saffron the whole truth. "And I need *you* with me," Callie admitted to her friend.

Callie had thought about buying the lodge on her own, but then she remembered those eighteen-year-old girls and she couldn't do it. Not without Saffron. Sure, it would be the best if all of her friends came along for the ride. Kenzie would bring the kind of business acumen their back of house would crave, Hazel's eye for design would always have the lodge at the height of style, and Laurel was the type of woman to persevere through any kind of storm, continuing to work when everyone else gave up around her, but for Callie, Saffron was the most important piece. The two had been best friends ever since kindergarten, and the dream, well, it just could not happen without Saffron. Callie couldn't imagine it.

"Call, you don't *need* anyone," Saffron said with a laugh, and Callie sometimes wished that were true. Her life would be a whole lot more simple if she didn't. Heck, she'd tried to not need anyone for years, lied to herself that that was the case, but now as a milestone birthday came nearer, Callie could no longer lie to herself. She needed her family. She needed her friends. More than that, she had a hollowness inside that she had a feeling only one kind of relationship could fill, the kind of relationship she'd ignored for most of her life, but Callie didn't have time to think about that at the moment. Those thoughts would plague her once again as she tried to fall asleep that night.

"I need you to do this with me," Callie said in a tone that she hoped Saffron would take seriously. "Do you remember when we drove out to the lodge and sat on the fence between the Caseys' vineyard and the lodge grounds?"

Saffron smiled at the image Callie knew was filling her mind. The vines on one side of wooden rails, the lush green lawn of the Rosebud Lodge on the other. The big, log building filling at least half of the gigantic yard with its shade as the sound of rockers creaking on the oversized front porch filled their ears.

"We made a promise, Saff," Callie said, and Saffron nodded.

"That was thirty years ago, Callie. A whole lot has changed," Saffron said before adding, "*We've* changed."

"But what really matters, that hasn't changed," Callie said, and she watched Saffron swallow. "We're still best friends. The lodge is still the heart of Rosebud. And it's dying, Saff. It would be like the start of all of this." Callie waved a hand behind her toward the kitchen. "Except we'd be bringing something to life that really matters to Rosebud. To the place we know and love."

Saffron frowned, but Callie knew her friend well enough to know that wasn't a bad sign. It just meant she was really thinking.

"And you'd get to do it with us, your girls. Not the douchebags you now call partners," Callie added with a grin, and Saffron chuckled.

"All of my money is tied up in the restaurant," Saffron said, and Callie nearly yelped with glee. She had her. Saffron was on board.

"I'll cover your portion until the sale goes through," Callie said.

"The guys won't make it easy," Saffron added.

"You've never liked easy," Callie replied, and Saffron threw her head back and laughed.

"I don't," Saffron said through her chuckles.

"So we're doing this?" Callie asked, her heart feeling lighter than it had in years. Her best friend was coming home. They were going to buy their lodge.

"On one condition," Saffron said.

"Anything," Callie said.

"You have to come to church with me every week. Because we know that now that I'm moving home, Mama Pierce will demand it of me," Saffron said with a grin that Callie could, ironically, only describe as *wicked*.

Callie shrugged. It was a small price to pay.

"Deal," Callie said as she stuck out her hand for Saffron to shake.

"Deal," Saffron repeated with a small shake of her head as if she couldn't believe she had actually given in. But she looked excited about it, and Callie was thrilled.

They were going to do this.

CHAPTER TWO

KENZIE THREW her purse onto one of the stools that sat at the island in her kitchen before kicking off the high heels that had plagued her feet all day and then pulling her long, dark hair out of the bun that had begun making her neck ache, running her fingers along her scalp.

"Kenz, is that you?" her husband Bryan asked as he entered the kitchen from their living room.

Kenzie had wanted more of an open concept space when they'd bought their condo in one of San Francisco's premiere high rises, but the designer of their condo had given the modern kitchen all four walls. Something about spatial recognition or other words that Kenzie didn't care to understand. The building gave Kenzie something she cared about far more than an open concept: it was just five minutes from her office, so she dealt with all four walls fairly happily. It wasn't like she was in her home all that often anyway. It was now after ten P.M. and she would have to be in her office before seven the next morning.

"Hey," Kenzie said as she took in her husband of ten years—his dark-brown eyes, wavy blond hair that he always kept extremely short, and hunky muscular arms. Kenzie had married well in every way. She gave him a lingering kiss before turning to the fridge to see it was full of Chinese takeout containers.

"Have I told you how much I love you?" Kenzie asked her husband who had to have ordered all of the extra takeout for her.

Bryan gave her a small smile before rounding the island to sit on one of the stools. Kenzie didn't like that small smile. Bryan's smiles were typically legendary. A small smile meant something was wrong. But Kenzie would deal with that after she got some food in her belly. She hadn't eaten since her late lunch eight hours before.

She opened a few containers to check their contents before throwing two into the microwave. She should have known Bryan would get her favorites.

"Did you have a good day?" Bryan asked, settling in for their evening discussion.

Kenzie and Bryan had met at work. Surprise, surprise, since Kenzie spent nearly all of her waking hours in her office building. She had just been named CFO of the small tech company she'd begun working for right out of college, and they had been in trouble. They were overspending and underperforming, so Kenzie and her CEO had decided to take drastic measures. They'd hired a consultant. And not just any consultant. Enter Bryan. The kind of consultant who cleaned house. He found what was working and what wasn't. The man was a genius at what he did. His reputation preceded him. And although the it had been a rough time on all of them, it had also been a time of rebirth for Kenzie's company. They thankfully hadn't had to let too many employees go, and now all of them who had stayed were thriving, and so was her firm. Thanks to Bryan.

Kenzie had also found out that Bryan had helped all those who had lost their jobs find new ones. That was when Kenzie had started falling for him. And they just clicked. They both loved their jobs and didn't have any plans for a family. Kenzie had found that to be a deal-breaker with most men. But she knew what she was good at. And being a mother wasn't it. Her friends Hazel and Laurel thrived in their roles as mothers, but Kenzie would make a mess of it. She knew she would. And botching up a child wasn't like botching up a job. There was no moving on. She would have ruined a human being. So Kenzie stuck with what she excelled in.

In the last five years, Bryan had begun to hire on consultants and train them to do what he had done for Kenzie's company. And then in the last year or more, Bryan had begun to work less, something he'd felt he'd needed to do for his sanity. He actually, these days, kept the hours of nine to five. Kenzie had been worried he'd ask her to do the same, but he hadn't. Because Bryan got her. He was her lobster, her partner for life, and he was a keeper. And not just because he ordered her favorite Chinese takeout.

"It was a day," Kenzie answered Bryan's earlier question. He didn't seem fazed that Kenzie's thoughts had wandered for a while before she'd answered him. Then again, they'd been married for ten years. By now, Bryan knew, if not understood, most of Kenzie's quirks. Wandering thoughts was a big one.

"Our quarter-end numbers weren't where the shareholders wanted to see them. So I spent the day placating irate investors and then trying to explain to Jeff how I would get our numbers back up," Kenzie said as she dug into her kung pao chicken. She smiled at Bryan because she knew he hated spice and therefore kung pao chicken. He'd ordered it just for her.

"The numbers were fine," Bryan said before lifting his glass of water. His hand seemed to twitch just as the cup reached his lips, and a bit of water spilled on his face and neck. Bryan wiped away the water but kept his attention on his wife.

"They were. But they dipped when they haven't dipped in

a while, and I guess I understand. Shareholders just care about the money," Kenzie said with a sigh. In the early years, this had all been so exciting to her. And sometimes it still was. But days like today, she was just tired. And a little sickened by how much money meant to some people. To some of the shareholders she'd dealt with that day, it definitely meant more than being gracious or even treating Kenzie like a human.

"I'm sorry," Bryan said, and Kenzie shrugged. It was just a bad day. Things would look better tomorrow, or maybe a couple of weeks from then. Kenzie was pretty sure she'd go in the next day to an inbox flooded with emails.

"How was your day?" Kenzie asked absently as she moved from kung pao to lemon chicken before realizing she didn't have any rice. She turned to the fridge to search for some rice. She was sure Bryan would have ordered some.

"Not great," Bryan said, and Kenzie remembered his small smile.

Thoughts of rice were forgotten as she turned to her husband.

"What happened?" Kenzie asked as she rounded the island and took a seat next to Bryan. The man was forever an optimist. Even in his line of work. Which wasn't easy. For him to admit a day wasn't great...well, Kenzie was afraid of what he would say next. "Was it one of your consultants?"

Bryan shook his head and then cleared his throat. His hands were beginning to twitch again, so he grabbed hold of the side of the island to steady them. Kenzie's heart stuttered a little more. What could be so bad?

"I went to the doctor today," Bryan said, and Kenzie froze. The doctor? Why hadn't Bryan told her he had a doctor's appointment?

"I've actually been going to the doctor for a few weeks,"

Bryan continued, and Kenzie felt her stomach turn as she gripped the island in the same manner Bryan was doing.

Bryan drew in a deep breath. "You know how I've been a bit more klutzy recently?" he asked, and she nodded.

When they'd first been dating and married, her husband had been the epitome of coordination. It drove Kenzie crazy that there was literally nothing physical the man couldn't do. She was the one who'd been rowing nearly all of her life, and Bryan, on his first try, had been a natural, and ever since, anytime she made the mistake of racing him, she was toast.

But recently, Bryan had tripped over his own feet a few times. And small things like the water spilling he'd just done. It wasn't exactly a common occurrence, but Kenzie had to admit she kind of appreciated her husband wasn't always the picture of grace.

"I went to my GP about a month ago because it seemed a little weird. I've always been pretty steady on my feet, and I figured I should get it checked out," Bryan said, and Kenzie felt her mouth drop open.

"A month ago?" Bryan had been going to the doctor for a *month*?

He nodded.

"But you didn't say anything?" Kenzie said, trying to think about the last month. How had she been so blind? The man she was married to had been going to the doctor for a month, and she hadn't seen anything out of the ordinary. In fact, when she looked back on the last month, almost all of her memories were in her office. Maybe that explained why she hadn't seen anything. She hadn't been here.

"I didn't want to scare you. In case it turned out to be nothing," Bryan said.

But he was telling her now. That meant it wasn't nothing.

Kenzie felt her stomach lurch, and she tried to keep her

body under control. She had to hear Bryan out. She had a feeling he had a whole lot more to say.

"They've been doing a few tests. So far we've gotten nothing conclusive," Bryan said the words slowly and patiently, causing Kenzie to calm until she really listened to the words. Nothing conclusive? After a month? That couldn't be good, could it? And if there was nothing conclusive but Bryan was still speaking to her about his appointment...what had happened?

"They think it could be ALS, Kenz," Bryan said softly, and Kenzie felt her spine shrivel.

ALS? She'd had a friend of a friend who'd endured the illness, and Kenzie had followed her journey carefully. The woman had since passed, because those with ALS didn't live long, did they? Kenzie didn't know much about the illness, but everything she did know rocked her very world.

"ALS?" she whispered.

Bryan nodded again before adding, "They don't know for sure. But that's what they are going to begin to look at. ALS is hard because there is no one definitive test that will tell us I have it. They have to rule out everything else, and if all that is left is ALS, surprise," Bryan choked over the last word. He'd always been terrible about making jokes at the wrong time, and this was definitely the wrong time.

Kenzie almost laughed at his attempt anyway until she realized just how cruel this surprise would be. "Are you okay?" she asked before even thinking about what she was asking. Of course he wasn't okay. "I mean..." Kenzie struggled to find the words. Maybe this was why Bryan had left her out of the loop. Kenzie thrived while working out puzzles in her business life, but throw her a curveball at home? She was sure to strike out.

"It's fine, Kenzie. I'm fine. At least I feel fine right now." Bryan didn't say what they both were thinking. He could very well not be fine at all. He could be the sickest he'd ever been.

"I'm more worried about you," he said, and Kenzie fought back all the emotions that threatened. Of course he was worried about her. This was her sweet Bry. But Kenzie couldn't give into the fears and tears. She could sift through her own feelings later. For now, she needed to be there for her dear husband. Who might have ALS.

"Bry, you should have called me as soon as you left your doctor's appointment," Kenzie said, thinking back on all the time she should have been there for Bryan, but she hadn't. Because he hadn't let her in. That stung. And as much as she understood why Bryan had left her in the dark, it was hard not to take it personally. Because it *was* personal.

"I knew your day was going to be hectic at best," Bryan said as he put a hand over Kenzie's to comfort her. She should have known he would use this moment to take care of her. He always took care of Kenzie. But it was time for those roles to be reversed.

"I would have taken your call," Kenzie said, and Bryan nodded.

"I know. But it would have been between the calls and emails from irate shareholders, and I couldn't do that to you," Bryan said, and Kenzie understood. Her work life was a mess on the best of days. Bryan had learned that the time he had with his wife was just those hours that she wasn't physically in the office. And how many hours was that daily? Eight, sometimes ten? That meant Kenzie was only giving a third of her life to the man she loved with all of her heart. A man she could be losing... Kenzie felt tears prick her eyes.

No. No falling apart. They didn't know anything yet.

Suddenly all of what Bryan had told her hit Kenzie so hard she literally shook in her chair. Her husband was sick, maybe even dying. And he didn't feel that kind of news was worthy of interrupting her day. Because she'd told him her priorities.

Work...and then everything else. But that wasn't right. Kenzie had never meant to put work as such a priority. It had just happened naturally over the years. And when Bryan had come into her life, she'd made him squeeze into the open spots. She hadn't made any room for him, other than in her heart. And Kenzie rarely let her heart decide how she lived her life.

But that had to change. It was going to change. How could she make it change?

"Kenz?" Bryan asked softly.

Kenzie squeezed her husband's hand, trying to tell him all she was feeling without any words. Words weren't coming to her just yet. She needed a plan.

She thought about cutting back on her hours, but she knew that could never happen in her current job. Keeping her position as her company's CFO meant working long and hard. It was what she had signed on for. There was no way to just up and say 'I'd like to work less.' She could imagine Jeff's response to that one. They all wished they could work less. But they had jobs to do. And they couldn't just do half of the work and think their company would thrive.

So that wouldn't work.

Could she leave her job? She swallowed. It wasn't that she loved it all that much. Especially after a day like today had been. But it was all she knew. She'd been working in the same space, the same company since she'd graduated from college nearly thirty years before. And that was the way she liked things. She liked order and consistency. And she absolutely hated change.

But a change was coming. And she had to decide how she would meet it.

Was her panic premature? Bryan could possibly have ALS. It could be other things as well. They'd need more tests. What if Kenzie quit her job and Bryan was fine?

But then she remembered that Bryan hadn't even felt he

could call her to interrupt her day with life-altering news. As long as she stayed at her current job, that would never change. And she couldn't do that to her husband. She couldn't do that to herself. She really was living just half a life. The half of life where she worked. Where was her time for enjoyment? For actually living? Her job was her hobby, her livelihood; she'd made it absolutely everything to her. And what did it give her? Some satisfaction and a really great income. But was that worth all she was putting into it?

If you had asked her ten years ago or even last year, she would have said yes immediately. But after this evening, after seeing her husband endure what he had alone? No. No, it wasn't worth it. She needed more out of life. She needed more time with Bry. More time for herself. And possibly a new job. She and Bryan had all that they needed when it came to money in investments, properties, and savings. Kenzie could quit that day and never need to work again. But she knew herself. Not having a place to go every day would drive her insane. It would drive Bryan insane.

But what kind of job could she find that wouldn't ask her to work the hours her job now was asking of her? Nothing in the city, that was for sure.

Nothing in the *city*...Kenzie's thoughts began to run wild. The pace of the city was too much for them. Too much for her right now. She needed to slow down. They both needed to slow down. Bryan had found a way to do so even while running his company, but Kenzie would never be able to do the same. Not here in their lives, the same ones they'd lived for the past ten years. They needed a big change if things were going to look different for them.

Kenzie began imagining rolling vineyards and massive lawns. Mature trees and small roads.

Rosebud. It was calling to her. Telling her that one specific change wouldn't be too much for her to handle. Going home.

Kenzie swallowed. Bryan had loved Rosebud the times she'd taken him there. Although her hometown was less than two hours up the coast, it felt a world away, and they'd only ever gone home on the few holidays Kenzie didn't go into work.

Bryan was from a similar small town in Washington State, but since his parents had both passed on, she hadn't been to his hometown in years. He hadn't wanted to return without his parents around. The place hadn't felt the same to him.

But Rosebud was the opposite for Kenzie. She'd always been able to breathe in the fresh air and feel like herself once again. Between her family and her best friends, the place called to her now more than ever. But would Bryan feel the same?

"You've been quiet for a long time," Bryan said, and Kenzie felt horrible. She was supposed to be trying to find a way to comfort Bryan, but her thoughts had drawn her away from him. However, she hoped her next words would change everything.

"How do you feel about Rosebud?" Kenzie asked, and Bryan frowned as he watched her.

"I've always loved your hometown," Bryan said slowly as if he were trying to catch up to what she was thinking.

"What if we moved there?"

Bryan's eyes went wide. He opened his mouth—she was sure to argue with her—but Kenzie needed him to know her thought process first. She was sure his objections had more to do with her than with himself, that was just who Bryan was, but she needed him to understand this would be for her as much as it would be for him. It would be for *them*. Allow both Bryan and Kenzie to live at a slower pace. To focus on them as they endured whatever fate might throw at them.

She put up a hand as Bryan said, "No, absolutely not."

"Hear me out, please?" she pleaded, and Bryan closed his

mouth, but showed he wasn't going to be easy to win over when he crossed his arms over his broad chest. The place where Kenzie loved to lay her head each night. Bryan was her rock. He had been ever since they met. But now she wanted to be strong for them. To find the right path for them.

"I've been working too much," she began.

Bryan barked out a single laugh. "That's the understatement of the year. But it's who you are."

Kenzie swallowed, hating how that sounded, but it *was* who she was. She worked. Hard, long hours. That was what she did. It was *all* she did. How had she gotten here? Life had just been moving on, getting more filled with work moment by moment, and Kenzie had never taken the time to see if that was what she really wanted. And before, maybe she had, but now? Now that Bryan could be sick?

Her priorities were messed up. And she needed to sort them out.

"It's not who I want to be." Kenzie twirled a piece of her muddy brown hair around a finger. Her hair had gotten long, but she'd been too busy with work to even schedule a hair appointment. She'd taken to dying her own hair, just to save time.

"It's not?" Bryan asked, looking as confused as he sounded. Kenzie didn't blame him.

She shook her head. "It's just...work kind of took over. And I let it, don't get me wrong. But I don't love it. At least not the way I used to. And definitely not the way I love you."

Bryan shook his head. "You had a bad day, Kenz. And then you came home to terrible news from your husband. You're shaken, that's all." He wrapped an arm around Kenzie's shoulders, but this time she was the one who shook her head.

"That's not it, Bry. It may have taken your news for me to notice anything outside of my ridiculous routine, but I haven't been happy. I've been surviving, even excelling at work, but it's my whole life."

"No, it's not. You've always got me," Bryan said as he tugged Kenzie closer to him, and she reveled in his warmth.

"I know. But do *you* have *me*?" She looked up at him, and he gave her a quizzical look. She loved it when his light brows lifted like that.

"You didn't feel you could call me. Or come into the office. Or ask me to come home early. When you got news from your doctor that you might have ALS. Bryan, it doesn't get much bigger than that. And yet, you felt you couldn't have me by your side. I'm not okay with that," Kenzie spoke with more vehemence than she meant to, but this wasn't right. Not just what the doctor had told Bryan, but their whole lives. It was all wrong. Except that she and Bry were meant to be together.

"But moving? We've lived here our whole marriage. Heck, our entire adult lives," Bryan said, and Kenzie nodded. They had. Kenzie had attended college in the city and then had never left. Bryan had gotten his first job on the other side of the city before building his own company from the ground up.

However, just because they'd always been here didn't mean it was right for them still.

"Do you love it here?" Kenzie asked, and she felt Bryan's body tighten beside hers. She doubted it was a question he'd asked himself in years. She knew she hadn't. But now that she thought about it, she didn't. She didn't love any of it. They lived in their supposed dream home, but Kenzie had really only chosen the place because it was a penthouse close to her office. How sad was that? As she looked at all of the modern straight lines, the dark countertops in the kitchen, the black state-of-the-art appliances, none of them would have been her choice. Their living room furniture had been chosen by a decorator who worked with the building, and Kenzie had barely even looked at the choices before signing off on them; she just hadn't had the time to care. And now she was left with a couch that hardly gave way when she sat on it and a picture frame that turned into a TV. Okay, that last part was cool, but she wouldn't have chosen it. Not for herself. She didn't watch TV. Neither did Bry. So they didn't need a TV that cost three times as much as her first car.

Their condo had too many rooms and no yard. So Kenzie didn't even have the dog she'd always dreamed of. Well, no yard and the fact that anything under her care would eventually starve. She didn't even have the time to keep a houseplant alive.

"I don't love it," Bryan said slowly. "But it's home."

"Is it?" Kenzie countered immediately. "I hate our bed," she blurted.

"What?" Bryan's quizzical brow was back.

"It's too soft. But I had my assistant choose it because who has time to go bed shopping? And the only guideline I gave her was that I wanted it to be king-sized. I didn't know I hated soft beds," Kenzie said, and Bryan began to laugh.

"We can get a new bed," he said through his laughter, and Kenzie shook her head.

"It's more than that," she said, causing Bryan's laughter to stop. "Nothing about this place is us. Heck, my office is homier because I spend more time there."

Understanding began to light Bryan's eyes.

"But this could be nothing," he said softly, and Kenzie understood that. The doctors were just looking at ALS as a possibility. It could be something way less severe. But Bryan's news had just been the instigating incident. Now that Kenzie was delving into parts of her she'd ignored for too long, she was seeing what she'd been blind to.

"I know," Kenzie responded in the same tone Bryan had used. "But I still want to move."

"You *want* to move?" Bryan said as he looked around the space they'd been dreaming of for years. They'd both been young, poor, and hungry in the city at one time. They'd shared their younger selves' aspirations with one another while they'd been dating, and this condo was the culmination of the two of them coming together. The dream they'd shared even before knowing each other.

"I think we need to move," Kenzie said, wishing she could speak as eloquently as she could deal with numbers. Hand her any spreadsheet, and Kenzie would thrive. But emotional discussions, she tended to shut down. And she didn't want to. Not this time.

"My job is too much. It's taken over everything." She looked up to meet Bryan's gaze.

"It's your dream position. You worked your tail off to get there," he said, and she smiled. Because she had. But now that she was living her aspiration, it wasn't all it had been cracked up to be.

"But I got it. And I worked it. And I proved I'm really good at what I do."

"You have," Bryan responded, and Kenzie smiled. Bryan had always been her number one cheerleader.

"It was what I needed. At a time in my life. But that time has passed, and I need something more." Kenzie tried to explain her swirling thoughts.

"More?" Bryan asked.

"More time," Kenzie finally said. "I want a multifaceted life," she explained, and she felt Bryan nod.

"So you can cut back on your hours, like I did," Bryan said, and Kenzie shook her head.

"My job isn't like yours. It's all or nothing."

"And you'll be okay with nothing?" Bryan asked, his dark eyes honed in on her light-blue ones.

No. She wouldn't. They both knew that. Suddenly, Kenzie remembered the text she'd gotten from Callie a few weeks before. She hadn't responded because she didn't know how to. The lodge was up for sale. Their lodge. The one they had, as young women, dreamed of owning someday. That was the kind of job Kenzie needed. Building something beautiful with people she loved, not trying to outrun other companies in a highly competitive sphere.

"The Rosebud Lodge," Kenzie blurted as Bryan continued to meet her gaze.

"The lodge your friends were talking about buying?" he asked.

Kenzie nodded.

"It's nothing like what you're doing now," Bryan said, his eyes boring into Kenzie as if he was trying to see into her soul.

"They'd put me in charge of the finances and back-of-house operations. So it's kind of like it," Kenzie said, sure that was Callie's plan. The woman was nothing if not resourceful. And Kenzie was a resource Callie would know just how to use.

"But in a small town," Bryan said.

"*My* small town," Kenzie corrected.

"Yes, your small town. The town you had to escape."

"Thirty years ago."

"And you want to go back?"

Kenzie nodded. She hadn't known how much she wanted this until now, this very conversation. But it was what she wanted more than anything. To move to a place she knew but had a slower pace. A place she could truly get to know her sweet husband and make him a priority. A place where she could see her parents consistently; a place where she'd get to work with people she loved.

She'd nearly erased that text because the dream had haunted her so badly. But it had seemed impossible. She had a job. She had a life. But now Kenzie could see why the text had shaken her so. It had awakened a craving she hadn't known she'd had. And Bryan's possible diagnosis was what she had needed to spur her to a place where she was ready to face that. This was exactly what she needed.

And there was that word. *She.* Kenzie suddenly realized that she'd made this all about her. The idea had started because she wanted to do this for them, for Bryan, but this was the way *she* thought it was best to deal with things. And Bryan had been fighting her. She'd been assuming he was fighting against the idea of moving to Rosebud for her, but what if it was for him? What if he didn't want to change their entire lives? Kenzie had always been selfish and self-serving, but this was a new low. Even for her.

"I'm so sorry," she burst out. "I've been making this all about me. When it's about you. How do I do that?"

Bryan chuckled as he pulled her close and kissed the top of her head.

"You've been thinking about me. Giving up all that you know, for me. Only you would call that making everything about you," Bryan said, forgiving her too quickly, the way he always did.

"But it's been about my way. I've been bulldozing." Kenzie had often been told she railroaded those around her into what she wanted. It made her a great businesswoman but not the best wife.

"I love Rosebud. I love the idea of slowing down. I've been wanting that for a few years. But you haven't. I can't stand the idea that you are turning your entire life upside down for a what if," Bryan said.

"So your only objection is that I might regret it?"

"You say it so easily, but, yes. It's a major objection."

"It is." Kenzie wanted to show Bryan she was taking this seriously. She was taking him seriously. "But I'm not changing my life for a what if. I'm changing it because that what if has made me re-evaluate everything."

"That's what I mean. My announcement spurred this. You are being driven emotionally," Bryan said, and Kenzie smiled.

"Exactly. I'm finally acknowledging my emotions. What more than just my work life needs," she said. Bryan scooted back on his chair as he held both of Kenzie's shoulders and met her eyes.

"Look at me," he said, and Kenzie met her husband's intense stare.

"This is what you want?" he asked.

Kenzie nodded.

"For you?" he asked.

"For us."

"That's not what I asked. What if I weren't here? What if I hadn't just dropped this bomb on you?"

"Then, no. I wouldn't be doing it," Kenzie said honestly.

Bryan dropped his arms. "So, no moving."

"Wrong," Kenzie replied. This time she put her arms on Bryan's strong shoulders.

"What?"

"Without you my life wouldn't be worth truly living and exploring. It's because of you that I care about anything other than my job. You make my life whole, Bry," Kenzie said as she allowed a single tear to fall. Kenzie didn't do emotions. Other than for Bryan and those she loved.

Kenzie watched Bryan's eyes tear up as well.

"Really?" he asked, and she knew what he was asking. Did she really want to uproot her entire life? Change everything they had? The woman who hated all change?

And Kenzie only had one answer to give.

"Absolutely."

CHAPTER THREE

HAZEL NEARLY GROWLED at the insurance rep she was on the phone with when he asked once again for her to explain her situation. She had been on the phone with four different representatives, and none of them had been able to complete the simple task of changing her name and address on her policy.

"I've moved. I would like to change the address on the policy for me and my children to my new address, and I also need to change my name," Hazel said, proud of how patient she sounded, considering the urge to roar was still strong.

"Change your name, Ma'am?" the man asked, and Hazel literally bit her lip to keep her growl in.

She drew in a deep breath and let go of her lip. "Yes."

"Do you have a form that certifies your change of name?" the man asked.

"Yes. And as I mentioned to your colleague before, I sent it in. You all should have it on record," Hazel knew her last few words were heavy with some of the rumble she had been trying to control, but she was beyond annoyed. What should have been a simple task had taken her hours, and she just really needed insurance. Her younger son was on medication for his depression, and she wasn't about to let that lapse because the insurance company couldn't figure things out.

"Oh, yes. I see it here. Did you get divorced, Ma'am?" the young man asked.

"Yes, sirree." Hazel knew the sarcasm was too much, but it was either that or she was gonna blow. She didn't think the young man would like the latter as well as the former.

"And you are still on your ex-husband's policy?" he asked.

This had been a question all three previous reps had asked as well.

"Yes."

Hazel did not feel the need to explain any more than that. To tell this kid from who-knew-where her entire life story. That she'd married a man right out of high school, one who had charmed her and written songs about her. His star had risen quickly, and Hazel's right along beside his. She was known as the prettiest muse in the country music world, and people loved snapping pics of her and her crooning husband. A couple of adorable baby boys had come along, completing their family. And all had looked perfect...on the outside. Hazel had felt her husband beginning to pull away years before. She had a special personality, as her mom liked to call it. She was strong-willed, to say the least, and her husband wasn't.

Her *ex*-husband.

Her fire had been what had drawn him to her, but he had found that standing next to the roaring flames could cause him to be burned. When Hazel got upset, she would rage. But it was that same fire that caused their passion to sizzle just as hot. However, after some time, the passion and her strength weren't worth what her husband liked to call Hazel's 'fits.'

So he'd asked her for a divorce. One that Hazel had seen coming, so she'd known what she needed. She wanted financial security for herself and her boys. And she wanted her boys with her, full-time. She wanted to go home to Rosebud, and she wanted her ex to provide them a home. With all of those needs fulfilled, Hazel was okay stepping aside for the new, pretty girl who would become her ex's muse. Hazel didn't want to stay with a man who didn't want her. Who wouldn't fight for them.

And that was why she was on the phone with this rep, once again practically begging for those two simple things to be changed. Nothing else had to be. Her ex's team had seen to that.

"We will need a notarized...."

Nope, nope, nope. This would never do. Hazel knew the man was just doing his job, but she was also pretty sure that he could pull more strings than he was admitting to. Sterling needed to see a therapist ASAP. The divorce may not have been hard on Hazel, but watching their family fall apart had been terrible for both of her boys. And this man was standing in the way of care she needed for her sweet boy.

Hazel let out her growl, startling the man into silence.

"My ex has turned in the paperwork. The first young woman I spoke to assured me that was the case. Then I sent in the information I needed for my change of address to a second young woman. Then it was the third rep who told me about the certified change of name form, and now I am speaking to you. There can be no more that you could possibly need from me. I have given you all but my firstborn. Now get this all figured out...now!"

Hazel heard movement on the other end of the line and wondered if she was going to be passed off yet again. The only upside to that was maybe she would finally be sent to a person who would complete her request.

She knew it wasn't completely vital for her to get this insurance seen through. Thankfully, her divorce settlement had left her with all she needed and more. But why would she waste an arm and a leg on seeing a doctor and getting medication when her ex was already paying for insurance that should cover both? Sterling was his son too, and Hazel knew the insurance company should provide for him. It just didn't seem to want to.

"Ma'am." The same young man was back. Hazel smiled in surprise. To come back instead of handing her off meant he had more backbone than most, and she approved.

"Yes?" Hazel said.

"Oh, uh..."

Hazel knew her pleasant tone must have startled him, and she suppressed a chuckle. She wasn't a monster.

"You were right. We have all that we need to make those changes. I'll send you an email with the details, but the changes have been made and you are free to look for a doctor in your area," the rep said, and Hazel grinned.

Finally. It had taken four calls in the week since she'd moved back to California, but it was done.

"Thank you," she said gratefully.

"Not a problem," the man responded, and Hazel said goodbye before hanging up.

Now back to the other million and one tasks she had to tackle since their move.

"Mom!" Hazel's oldest son, Chase, called out as he skidded in his socks past the dining room where she sat.

"Yes?" Hazel asked, grateful that her annoyance at the insurance company had subsided. The last thing she needed when going into a Chase interaction was already pent-up frustration.

"Where's my skateboard?" he asked, his dark brows nearly disappearing in his head full of blond curls.

Hazel didn't love that her oldest was growing his hair out. She did love his blond curls, but now stray ones were beginning to cover his beautiful green eyes and Chase was constantly batting at them. Hazel knew it was a look, all the teens were doing it, but she was not a fan.

"Did you unpack your room?" Hazel countered. They'd been in their new home in Rosebud for over a week now, and although the movers had done most of the heavy lifting and Hazel had taken over unpacking all of the common areas on her own in addition to her bedroom, she'd asked each of her boys to do one thing. Their rooms. That was it. But it seemed too heavy a task, especially for Chase. As far as she knew, he hadn't even started yet.

"We aren't supposed to answer a question with a question," Chase spouted a rule Hazel's ex, Wells, had instilled in the boys when they were young.

"Your dad's rules don't apply to me," Hazel said, and then realized this probably wasn't her finest parenting moment. She sounded as trite as her teenagers.

But then again, wasn't a good parent never supposed to back down? Now that she'd said what she'd said, she had to follow through, right? Besides, what she'd said was true. If she was the mom and had to ask a question, she'd ask a question. But the tone she'd used could be worked on a bit.

Parenting had been a whole lot easier with Wells around. The man had made a lousy husband these past few years, but he'd always been an excellent father. Hazel felt a twinge of guilt at taking her boys away from said good father. But she hadn't wanted them traipsing across the country every other week between her and Wells, and she'd needed to come home to Rosebud. It was the only place she'd felt safe after her life had unraveled.

Because as much as her divorce didn't affect her in the same soul-crushing way it seemed to affect some other women, her life was still turned upside down by it. She was no longer Mrs. Wells Harrington, the belle of the country music world. She'd been cast aside by one of the greats, and Nashville supported their greats. Meaning if Wells set her aside, so would they all.

Hazel couldn't stay there and be treated in the way she'd seen so many exes endure. So she'd come to the one place she knew would always take her back with open arms. Rosebud.

And she'd demanded having her boys with her full-time. She knew Wells had only given in to her requirement for full custody because he felt guilty. Even though they'd been growing apart for years, he'd initiated divorce proceedings. And after seeing his new girlfriend post a picture of the two of them on social media the second Hazel left Nashville, she could see how he had finally grown the nerve to pull the plug on their dying marriage. Hazel was more than a trifle annoyed at herself that she hadn't done it. She had always been the decisive one in their relationship, but then again, she should be proud that she'd only quit on their family after Wells had done so. Granted, she would never quit on her boys, just on the unit she'd created with Wells.

"That's a bunch of...." Chase responded in the exact way Hazel had known he would. She really needed to not be so flippant with her words if she wanted to have a conversation with Chase that didn't end in an argument. She had to be more careful now that Wells wasn't around to talk Chase down when he and Hazel got upset with one another.

"If the next word you were planning on saying was a curse word, I'd rethink that," Hazel said firmly, using the careful wording and tone she should have from the very beginning. Her chastisement still caused Chase to bristle. However, Hazel wouldn't back down. Chase didn't have to like her, he just had to respect her.

Chase reminded her a whole lot of herself at that age. All teenage rebellion with little thought behind it. Wells had been the calm hand that Chase had needed while growing up, but now with Wells gone, Hazel wasn't sure how to raise her fiery son. Especially because she was still pretty fiery as well.

"BS," Chase finished and Hazel wasn't exactly delighted with his word choice but it was better than it could have been, so she let it go. For now. Wells had told her the secret to dealing with Chase was picking the right battle, but honestly, she wasn't sure how to do that. They all seemed important. At least in her book.

Hazel didn't miss her husband but she did miss co-parenting. She began to wonder if maybe she could hire one. Wasn't it possible to find just about anything on the internet these days?

"I'm your mother, Chase. Why would the rules for the children apply to me?" Hazel asked, and she raised her dark brow, nearly identical to Chase's. Not only were their temperaments alike, Hazel had given her own wild blonde curls and olive-green eyes to her son. Whereas Sterling could have been a replica of his father with his black hair and soulful brown eyes.

"Because as my role model, you should be modeling what you preach instead of just spouting words," Chase said as he leaned against the frame of the entryway of the formal dining room.

This very space that had seemed useless when Hazel had toured the place and had almost kept her from buying their new home had somehow become her haven. She hadn't realized she'd appreciate having this area just off the front door and away from the main living area. It was the perfect spot for her to reprimand her child and make unwanted calls to insurance reps. She doubted they'd have many, if any, formal gatherings the way the space was intended to be used, because her huge dining table in the eating area off the kitchen sufficed for any type of meal. Especially since it was connected to the open concept kitchen that flowed right into the family room and made that area excellent for entertaining. But this place, formerly a parlor, with its bright, white walls and crown molding, was growing on her.

Hazel reviewed the words her son had spoken and then

regretted taking him to therapy. Chase hadn't really needed it at the time, but because Sterling had started to go, Hazel had thought it would be a good idea for all of them to go with him. She didn't like having one brother do something the other didn't. And honestly, she didn't really regret taking Chase to therapy. She just regretted the way the sweet therapist's words could come back to bite her in the bottom.

"One, I doubt Doctor Smith would appreciate his words being used as a weapon," Hazel tried not to smile as she also remembered the teachings of the man who had helped them to have more harmony in their home. "But two, you're right. I should be modeling the behavior I expect in this home. However, I don't think your dad's rules should apply in our new home."

Hazel regretted the words as soon as she spoke them. She had been so focused on the one rule Chase had accused her of not following that she had forgotten there were quite a few of Wells' rules that she wanted to keep as the standard in her home. Like keeping their speech respectful or finishing their chores before dinner. Wells may have been a country music superstar, but the man had been just about as hands-on as any dad Hazel had ever witnessed. At least when he wasn't out on tour. Even when Wells had to work long hours creating a new album, he often took the boys with him to the studio, or when that wasn't possible, he'd set aside chunks of time to spend with them doing their favorite activities. Basketball or skateboarding for Chase and playing video games with Sterling.

"So now we're just going to stop following Dad's rules?" Chase asked, and Hazel was about to answer when he kept on going. "I get it, Mom. You hate him. He left you, and you're angry. But isn't it enough you took us away from him to this pit stop in the middle of nowhere; do you really have to pretend like he never even existed?" Chase practically shouted the last words, and Hazel bit back what she wanted to say. Throttled back her fury. And tried to think about what words would bring the resolution both she and Chase wanted. She wanted him to clean his room, and he wanted his skateboard. Right? Or was that even what this was all about anymore? Hazel wasn't sure; she didn't completely understand where their conversation had gone, but she decided to focus on those goals.

"I will tell you where your skateboard is after you've unpacked at least a third of your room," Hazel said, proud of the calm way she'd spoken each word.

"And now you're ignoring me?" Chase shouted, and Hazel wanted to throw her arms up in defeat. But she didn't.

"You wanted your skateboard," Hazel responded, and she knew her voice wasn't quite so calm anymore. But she couldn't allow Chase to get under her skin. She couldn't lose control. Not when there was no one left to play referee.

"I want to know why you want to completely scrub any and all memories of Dad out of our life. You can't do that, you know. Our memories are ours," Chase pushed.

Hazel felt an ache in her heart for her poor boy. Was that what she'd been doing? She didn't mean to. Sure, she was trying to prove that none of them had any need for Wells in their lives. Not after he'd discarded her. She could live alone. Parent alone. Thrive alone. But she shouldn't be trying to make her boys forget their dad. She didn't want that.

"I'm sorry if that's what I'm doing," Hazel said, and Chase rolled his eyes. At her sincere apology. Why the nerve of that...Hazel drew in a deep breath.

"If that's what you're doing. Of course it's what you're doing, Mom. You took us away from him and Nashville, the place we've called home for our entire lives, and now you won't even put up any pictures of him. Whenever I ask when I'm going to get to go home and see him, you ignore me or put me off. And now you won't even keep his rules?" Chase threw his arms in the air and stomped out of the room.

Hazel thought about going after him—their conversation was long from done—but some time apart would probably be helpful. She wasn't sure how to respond to all Chase had accused her of.

Was she being selfish? Keeping the boys from their dad? It wasn't like they were never going to visit him. She was planning a trip as soon as that summer. Taking full custody wasn't about keeping her sons away from their father. It had been about control. If Wells had partial custody of their children, the judge would have ordered the time spent in each home. Wells could demand things of Hazel that she wasn't comfortable giving. So this way was easier. She could deem when visits would happen, make sure school wasn't interrupted, and most of all, that the boys weren't taken away from her when they needed her. They were her children; she knew what was best for them more than a judge or even their father.

No, she'd made the right choice. Wells had seemed to understand it as well, since he'd ended up giving in to her. He knew she had been angry, but Wells also knew that Hazel's anger fizzled away quite quickly, and when it did, she was often levelheaded and almost always fair. If he'd really wanted to talk her out of full custody, he could have. But he hadn't. Meaning he had agreed that this was what was best for their boys. He knew Hazel would make the best choices when it came to their boys, because at the heart of everything, she would sacrifice anything for her children's safety, security, and well-being. And if that well-being meant they needed time with their father, she'd give it.

But the one thing she wouldn't question was moving her little family back to Rosebud. Nashville was Wells's town, the place where he was nearly worshipped. And maybe the one good thing to come out of the divorce already was that her boys would no longer be raised in his shadow. Sure, even those in Rosebud knew who Wells was, his star shone so bright, but it wasn't the way it had been in Nashville, with the entire town ready to cater to Wells's every need. Her boys were becoming too accustomed to being treated like royalty, and they needed some small-town humility in, what had Chase called it, this pit stop to nowhere?

Although that wasn't anywhere near a fair assessment. Rosebud was a small town, but it was just a couple of hours outside of San Francisco and even closer to the beach. It was a gorgeous place that people flocked to at all times of the year. Not quite the bleak picture Chase painted, but Hazel didn't blame him. She'd had the same sorts of feelings when she was sixteen. It was why she'd left the summer after high school and then a few years later had gotten married to a man who would take her all over the world.

"Hey, Mom," the quiet voice of her shy, younger son came from the same spot his larger-than-life brother had occupied moments before. The contrast between them was drastic, and yet Hazel's love for them couldn't be any more similar.

"Hi, Sweets," Hazel said as she pushed the insurance paperwork that still sat in front of her across the table. If she never had to look at that stuff again, it would be too soon.

"Chase didn't mean to get so angry at you," Sterling said, and Hazel saw what he was doing immediately, because it was what Wells had done for years. And she would not allow her son to do the same. That wasn't his job. It was hers. She just needed to get better at it.

"I know," Hazel said as she motioned to the chair beside her and Sterling took the seat. "And I see what you're trying to do, but you don't need to. Chase and I will be fine. We blow up, but I know he loves me. And he sure as heck better know that I love him," she said with a grin, and Sterling responded by giving her the same smile. His hair and eyes might be all his father, but Sterling had her smile.

"We'll be okay?" Sterling asked, and Hazel nodded as she pulled Sterling's chair closer so that she could put an arm around him. At thirteen, her younger son was just getting beyond the years where he was willing to cuddle up to his mom, but Hazel was okay with that. He didn't have to be willing, but she'd still hug him just the same. He'd always be her little boy.

"I know these past few months have been crazy. They haven't been fair to you or your brother. You two are paying for mistakes me and your dad made. But I love you. And Dad loves you."

"Even though you have full custody?" Sterling asked, and Hazel wasn't sure how her son knew about that. She and Wells had been careful about what they'd said in front of the kids, and they'd made sure to tell them nothing about the custody arrangement. They'd just said that the boys would be living with Hazel for the time being. But since Sterling had brought it up, she had to put any of his concerns to rest.

"You've seen how crazy bullheaded I can be," Hazel said, and Sterling laughed.

Good.

"Your father didn't stand a chance when I got it in my head that I needed to have full custody of you boys. It has nothing to do with your father loving you any less and everything to do with me loving you two more than life itself. Do you understand that?" Hazel asked, and Sterling nodded.

"But why didn't Dad at least try to keep us?" Sterling asked.

Hazel pulled him in closer. "Oh, he wanted to. But in the end, I think he still loves me a little bit. Or at least cares about me enough to want to see me happy. And he knew the only way I'd feel any kind of happiness after our divorce was if I had full custody of the two of you. You two are our worlds. Still. Your dad and I only speak when it's about the two of you, and it's the only time we agree. We both want what is best for you. So much," Hazel said before dropping a kiss on the top of Sterling's head. She was pretty sure he wasn't going to like that but she had to do it.

Sure enough, that kiss caused Sterling to sit up and pull away from Hazel's grasp, but she was pretty sure her hug and kiss had accomplished what she'd needed them to. Sterling now felt safe and secure in his new home. And he'd hopefully begin to feel that way about their new family dynamic.

"Mom?" Sterling asked, pulling Hazel from her thoughts.

"Hm?" Hazel answered as she met Sterling's brown eyes.

"What are you going to do now?" he asked, and Hazel cocked her head in confusion.

"Like right now?" Hazel asked as she looked at the time and realized she should get started on dinner. During her time as Wells's wife, Hazel had hardly ever cleaned, but she had cooked. It was her one way of feeling like she was being the homemaker she'd been raised to be. Not that her mom would have been upset if Hazel had decided to work outside of the home, heck, Hazel's mom had had a job for a few years while she'd been growing up, but her mom had been the epitome of the 'mom that made their house a home'. And Hazel had wanted to do that for her own children. And cooking had been her way of doing so. Although she hadn't ever really been cut out for cleaning. In fact, she had interviews with a few cleaning services lined up during the rest of that week.

"I was planning to get started on dinner," Hazel said when Sterling began to shake his head.

"I mean for work. You know. Since you won't be working with Dad's charity anymore," Sterling said, his cute face creased with worry lines that were much too mature for his young skin.

Hazel should have known Sterling would have overheard at least some of her conversation with her mother the day before. She'd made every attempt to be quiet, but her mother's voice tended to carry. They'd sat right at that very table and had attempted to map out Hazel's future. But she hadn't been ready. It felt like there were so many bits and bobs to finish around the house first. And now that she was a single mom, she was wondering if she should just stay home. Dedicate herself full-time to parenting. She knew she was blessed to be in a position to do so even after the divorce. At least for a few years, maybe until Sterling graduated from high school. And then she really should find a job. If she pinched every penny, she probably would be able to live on her divorce settlement for the rest of her life, but Hazel didn't want to have to pinch. Not when she wanted to take trips and make memories with her boys. Not when she was considering a cleaning service. So she would have to work. But she didn't have to start that very day.

"Are you worried about that?" Hazel asked Sterling and then realized it was a silly question. Sterling worried about everything.

"I know you loved the work you did with Young and Free," Sterling spoke about the nonprofit Hazel had worked with for the last five years, the one that had been founded by Wells. Hazel had loved helping decorate the homes they'd built for the less fortunate of Nashville. With the move, it hadn't made sense for her to stay on. But not doing the work anymore did leave a hole in her life. Still, she had a feeling her days would be pretty dang full just caring for her boys.

"I do. I did," Hazel corrected, and Sterling scrunched his nose. She almost laughed at the face her boy used to make even as a baby, but stopped when she realized how serious of a conversation this was for him.

"And have you noticed you and Chase have been fighting a

lot more?" Sterling asked, and that caused Hazel to think. *Had* she and Chase been fighting more? She guessed maybe they were. Although it was to be expected, wasn't it? Chase was going through a hard time, and he didn't have the easiest time expressing his emotions. Then again, neither did Hazel. It was a great thing for all of them that their insurance would allow for each of them to see a therapist again soon.

"I guess we have," Hazel admitted.

"Do you like fighting with Chase?" Sterling asked, and Hazel shook her head immediately.

"So you want to stop?" Sterling asked, and Hazel nodded, though she was pretty sure she must have had a puzzled look on her face. Where was Sterling going with this?

"Maybe you should work," Sterling suggested, and now Hazel knew she had a puzzled look on her face.

"Work?" Hazel asked.

Sterling nodded. "Doctor Smith said when we lose a part of ourselves, we tend to feel unfulfilled and ornery. Maybe you feel unfulfilled because you aren't working?"

Hazel was about to say she was pretty sure her fighting with Chase had less to do with her and everything to do with Chase but clamped her lips shut. That wouldn't be fair. It took two to fight. Could Sterling be right?

Hazel did feel like she was running on empty at all times, but that was because she was so busy, right? The move had worn her out, and now she was dealing with putting their lives back together. It was a lot for one person. The last thing she needed was more on her plate. That was why she hadn't responded to the text Callie had sent her about buying the lodge. The last thing Hazel needed was a project or a job...right?

"I know you love us, Mom. And I know you're busy because of the move. But what about when that all dies down? When all you have left is me and Chase? Chase will be moving out in two years and then you'll just have me." Sterling swallowed, and Hazel knew her boy. He was worried not only for her but for the pressure it would be on the two of them for Sterling to be her whole world. Of course, while she was busy unpacking the rooms of their house, Sterling had spent time unpacking their lives. And he had seen the future in a way she hadn't tried to yet. He really was wise beyond his years.

"You're right, my smart boy," Hazel said as she thought about pulling him in for another hug, but Sterling didn't seem to need it so she didn't. She was trying to find the balance of affection that a mom of a teenaged boy should have. It wasn't easy, but she was working on reading their cues. She didn't want to smother them, but she had to love on them.

"So you'll look for something?" Sterling asked hopefully, and she heard the other question he wasn't asking. Would she do everything in her power to help keep the harmony of their home? To stay out of Chase's hair so that maybe they could attempt to get along? Because although that last argument hadn't been an example of one, many of the disagreements she and Chase had had since the move were just because they were in proximity to one another nearly all day every day. The boys would be starting school in a few days, so that should help, but Sterling was right. Hazel shouldn't be putting all of her focus on just her two boys. It would be too much. At least for the three of them. Maybe other moms in this situation should stay home full-time, but it wouldn't be right for her and their little family.

"I might already have something," Hazel said, realizing that she wanted to run the idea past someone before accepting Callie's proposal. She knew that Sterling would appreciate being given a vote on whether Hazel should buy into the lodge. She also knew that Chase couldn't have cared less.

"Really?" Sterling's eyes lit with hope. The boy, no, he was a young man now, really was thirteen going on forty-five. Hazel sure hoped her going back to work would help Sterling to feel a little less pressure. Feel a little more like a teenager.

"Do you remember my friend Callie?" Hazel asked, and Sterling nodded. He hadn't had tons of contact with Hazel's best friends from high school, but he'd met them a few times and knew that Hazel was on the phone with at least one of them each month.

"She wants us to buy a lodge," Hazel said, and Sterling smiled.

"Like a hotel?" he asked, and Hazel nodded.

"A smaller one, but yeah. It's actually pretty large for a lodge. It's two stories tall and made of the most beautiful brown logs. There are windows and glass panes all along the front of it so it looks like it glitters in the setting sun. It has a gorgeous little rock lined pond in front of it...."

"There are a lot of those here," Sterling interrupted, and Hazel laughed.

"There are. And it even has a huge, beautiful pool."

"Does it have a spa?" Sterling asked the question Hazel typically asked about every place they'd ever stayed as a family.

Hazel laughed again. "Of course it does," she responded as she ruffled Sterling's hair.

"How would you buy it?" Sterling asked a logistics question. A Sterling move for sure.

"There are five of us. We'd each put in some money, and then we'd ask a bank for a loan for the rest of it."

Sterling nodded again as he took in the facts.

"What would you do at the lodge?"

"Decorate. The place is a little run-down right now; the owners haven't put much money into it recently, but that just means more fun for me."

"That sounds literally perfect. Why haven't you already told Callie yes?" Sterling asked, his eyes wide, and Hazel smiled.

Why hadn't she? Because she was worried it would be too much, but Sterling was right. If she focused solely on her two boys, she would go crazy. She'd drive them crazy.

"I guess I should," Hazel said, and Sterling nodded.

"No guessing about it. Text her now, Mom," Sterling commanded, and Hazel swallowed her chuckle so that Sterling wouldn't think she was laughing at him. But he was right. Smart kid that he was. She needed to text Callie now.

CHAPTER FOUR

CALLIE SAT ALONE at the table she'd reserved for herself and her friends in one of Rosebud's Italian restaurants. She smiled as she remembered all of the evenings she and her friends had spent there, at Spago. It was their go-to spot before every special event during high school. They'd come here with their dates before all four homecomings, and then again for their dinner before senior prom. The only reason they hadn't come for junior prom was because Kenzie's boyfriend at the time had rallied hard for a burger joint instead and they'd given in. Elbow-deep in greasy burgers, working hard to keep their precious dresses clean, the girls had decided they would never make that mistake again.

So this location felt right when it came to a place they should gather to decide their future together. Well, at least the future for most of them. Callie had just gotten a text from Laurel that she was out. She hadn't given much of an excuse, other than that it wasn't a good time for her. But Callie hadn't pressed. She got it or at least she tried to. They couldn't have predicted, that summer when they were all eighteen, that this would be the time for them to pounce. But it was. So Callie was so glad at least four of them were in. She could imagine no better partnership.

"Callie!" their very own blonde bombshell called out from the door where she'd entered. Nearly every male in the restaurant took a moment to appreciate the beauty that was Hazel before going back to their meals or the waiters back to their jobs.

Callie chuckled. Hazel seemed to just grow more beautiful with age. Which wasn't fair considering she had been a knockout thirty years ago. But some things just weren't fair. Callie used to feel insecure, since as the only other blonde in their group of friends, she constantly felt compared to Hazel and knew she was found lacking. But by the time they all reached high school, Callie had grown out of her insecurities and realized that, yes, Hazel was gorgeous. But no one cared that Callie wasn't as beautiful. She had her own strengths that she had learned to cultivate.

"It's been way too long," Hazel said as Callie stood to give her friend a hug. Although it had been months since Callie had seen her friend, Callie and Laurel probably got to see Hazel the most out of their group of friends because the two of them had stayed in Rosebud since graduation. But even they only saw Hazel every year or so. They probably would have seen her even less if it weren't for her joining her ex, Wells, whenever his tours came anywhere near Rosebud.

But even though Callie and Laurel saw Hazel the most, she knew that Hazel and Kenzie had a special bond, kind of the way she and Saffron did. Maybe it was because they were the ones to leave Rosebud the moment their last summer together ended, or maybe it was just because the best person to deal with Hazel's fire was their very own ice queen, Kenzie. However, anyone who really knew Kenzie didn't believe for a minute she was the frozen persona those who didn't like her made her out to be. But whatever the case, Hazel and Kenzie were close. Closer than anyone would expect, considering they hadn't lived in the same state in thirty years.

Callie pulled away from Hazel to see Kenzie had joined them and Saffron was just coming in the front door.

As Hazel moved to hug Kenzie, Callie took in her raven-haired friend, wanting to see if the newest stresses in her life were taking a toll on her. Kenzie had told them a little about what she and her husband were up against, how she needed to move home to slow down her life, but Callie knew Kenzie had probably kept most of the details close to her chest. It was just the way she was, and Callie didn't blame her. Kenzie's sometimes cold demeanor had served her well in the business world. Not that she was ever that way with her friends, but she had wielded it against pervy high school boys, and it had earned her the moniker of ice queen. Which Kenzie sometimes wore proudly.

But considering the mess in Kenzie's life, she didn't look any worse for wear. In fact, she actually appeared years younger than when Callie had last seen her, with her long black hair in a loose braid instead of its typical severe bun, plus she was actually wearing jeans. Callie was pretty sure the last time she had seen Kenzie not in business attire was back in high school. Callie did notice bags under Kenzie's eyes, which indicated she probably hadn't been sleeping well, but that was to be expected.

Saffron joined them just as Kenzie moved to Callie to hug her, and then, only after hugs were exchanged by all, did the four of them sit down around the table.

Callie's eyes moved from friend to friend. Kenzie's pale skin was the complete opposite of Saffron's milk-chocolate complexion. Callie and Hazel were somewhere in the middle, and if Laurel were there, she would truly round them out. Their last friend was Japanese-American, and although her skin wasn't near the deep hue Saffron's was, Laurel did get very tan in the summer. Something Callie was forever jealous of.

"I swear this place hasn't changed," Hazel said as she looked around the restaurant, taking in the maps of the different parts of Italy along with pictures of many Italian vineyards.

"It was actually heavily renovated a few years ago. But they wanted to keep the same feel," Callie said with a smile, and Hazel laughed.

"Well, they achieved that," Hazel responded, and the women all began to giggle. It was inevitable. When they got together, they reverted to the girls they were back in high school. Well, hopefully not completely, considering they were now going into business together. Callie hoped they could be more responsible, mature versions of those fun girls.

"Well, if it isn't the Rosebud Girls." A male voice caused all of the women at the table to look toward the kitchen, where a man was walking to their table.

"Allen Patterson?" Kenzie asked, and the man in question nodded.

He was the very boyfriend of Kenzie's who'd once insisted on the burger joint. Now, irony of all ironies? He owned Spago.

"That would be me," Allen said with a grin as he looked around the table. "But it looks like you're missing one?"

Saffron nodded as Callie began to realize that would be a question they'd probably get a lot. Everyone knew the Rosebud girls included Laurel, and yet, she wouldn't be involved in the venture with them. That made Callie equal parts sad and confused. She really would need to get a better explanation out of Laurel the next time she saw her. If only to be able to answer the questions that would surely be coming her way.

"And how have you been, Allen?" Hazel asked, and the man looked like a deer in the headlights.

Callie chuckled softly as Kenzie shot her a smirk. Hazel still had the same power she'd always had over the male population of Rosebud.

"Good," Allen cleared his throat. "Great. I mean, I own this place." And Callie swore the man was puffing out his chest.

"With your wife, I hear?" Callie added, and Allen's chest deflated.

"Right, yes. With my beautiful wife," Allen said as if recollecting that he was in fact a nearly fifty-year-old man with a wife and children, not the high school boy who had crushed on Hazel. According to Kenzie, that was why she'd broken up with him.

"So are you three back in town?" Allen asked everyone but Callie, and all three nodded, but offered no explanations. Although Allen had to know what had incited Hazel's move home. The news of Hazel's amicable divorce had made every newspaper, entertainment site, and online blog for days. No one could have missed that.

"For good?" Allen asked, and Callie sent a look around the table before she spoke.

"At least for now," Callie said, deciding not to divulge their plans to buy the lodge. It would be all over town soon enough, but Callie hoped that no one would leak news about their offer before she could get it in to the sellers. She didn't want the current owners counting on their offer, nor did she want others to get wind of what they were doing and beat her to it.

"That look, the one you sent the rest of the girls. That meant something, right?" Allen asked Callie, and all four women shrugged at the same time.

"It did," Allen said mostly to himself with a smile. "The Rosebud girls are back."

He paused, looking at each of the women before adding, "I'll send your waiter over. But it's good to have you all home."

Allen left, and the four women burst out into laughter. Not

because anything that had happened was particularly funny, but it was kind of weird to be called the Rosebud girls again, considering their girlhood was long gone and the interaction had been a bit stilted...okay, maybe the whole thing *had* been amusing. But Callie shushed her friends before Allen came out of the kitchen to investigate. She didn't want the man to feel like they were all laughing at him. It was more that they were laughing about what it felt like for most of them to be together again.

The waiter came over to take their orders, Saffron questioning him about every ingredient in the dishes she was interested in, and then it was time to get to business.

"I've drawn each of us up a contract," Callie said as she handed out the envelopes she'd been keeping in her large purse. She'd tried the briefcase look for a few years but decided it didn't suit her. So instead, Callie walked around with a purse nearly half her size. And she loved it. Not only because it served its purpose, but Callie got to write off the gorgeous bag as a business expense.

Hazel pulled hers out of the envelope immediately, seeming to pour over every word, while Kenzie did the same but more slowly and Saffron just stared at the envelope.

"I swear it won't bite," Callie promised, but Saffron continued to stare.

"It's just a big moment, ya know?" Saffron said, and the other women must have been listening while reading because they nodded.

"Who would have thought Callie, of all people, would be the one to draw up our contract when we decided to buy this thing?" Saffron said, making Hazel and Kenzie laugh.

"This coming from the woman who begged me to be by her side as she drew up a contract with her partners," Callie teased, and Hazel laughed.

"You know what I mean," Saffron said, and Callie did. This

was what came from hanging out with people who had known each other since their very first day of kindergarten.

"Come on, Cal. We love you, but your *grades*," Kenzie said, and Hazel continued to laugh.

"Even my C's were better than most of your grades," Hazel added, and Callie had to join the laughter. Her friends would have never teased her about her grades back in high school. Even though Callie had worked her hardest, she just couldn't seem to test well on the concepts the way everyone else would. She swore she understood things, but then she'd fail nearly every test. Her saving grace was the projects and extra credit work that teachers offered. She learned later in life that she had a form of dyslexia. She read just fine, but she had a terrible time retaining information. Especially when she did things like cram for a test. Now, she knew all it would take was a few of her memory games or some more time and she could retain just about anything. But back then, it had been one of her sorest trials. Although, she couldn't be too sad about it. Getting terrible grades in high school had kept her from going the traditional route of college and instead jumping right into a job in real estate. She could never be grateful enough to Mrs. Coolidge, who'd shown her the ropes in her real estate office, until Callie was outselling even the veterans and her mentor. So her high school grades were no longer a sore spot. They had been a stepping stone to her success.

"Yeah, yeah. Laugh it up," Callie said through her own laughter.

Saffron and Hazel continued laughing, but Kenzie shot Callie a look of concern. Count on the ice queen to worry about Callie's feelings. Kenzie did sometimes get so wrapped up in her work and life that she didn't notice these things, but when she did, she was more fairytale princess than icy villain. But Kenzie was okay with the misconception, so Callie didn't work too hard to correct it. Callie figured the people who believed that about Kenzie were the sad people who didn't truly try to get to know her friend.

"I'm fine," Callie mouthed, and Kenzie smiled just as their entrees were served.

"And to quell any of your concerns, I did have a lawyer finish drafting this thing," Callie said as she pointed to the documents all three women held.

"Beauty and brains. I always knew she'd go far," Hazel said with a wink before turning back to her food and reading.

Lunch was a pretty silent affair as the women looked over the contracts between taking bites of their delicious pastas and pizzas. Even Saffron, chef and critic that she was, had to compliment her primavera.

But after what felt like forever, Kenzie looked up at Callie with a smile. The other two were just seconds behind.

"Looks good to me," Kenzie said as Saffron nodded in agreement.

"Is the buy-in amount a concern to anyone?" Callie asked, not wanting any of her friends to feel they were contributing more than they could afford. She had split the down payment of their offer four ways and then planned on getting a loan for the rest of the amount, but if the money would be a hardship to any one of them, Callie would be happy to pitch in. It's what one did for their sisters.

Hazel and Kenzie shook their heads as Saffron looked around the group.

"I made the terms of our loan clear in your contract," Callie said to Saffron, who raised an eyebrow.

"I know. Basically, you give me the money as long as I need it. And I can pay you back whenever, without interest. This isn't the way you always do business, is it?" Saffron asked with a teasing smirk.

"Hey. If you don't like the terms, I can always change them. Sixteen percent interest?" Callie teased right back.

"You are a shark," Saffron countered, and all of the women laughed again. That was another thing Callie was looking forward to in the coming year: the laughter, even if there would be some tears mixed in.

"I'm glad you outlined the terms clearly. I know it's always suggested not to go into business with friends, but I can't imagine doing this with anyone else," Hazel said, and Callie nodded. She felt the same way.

"Callie, you are pretty much a genius," Kenzie added as Saffron and Hazel nodded in agreement. "This contract covers everything, but I still feel like we can keep our friendship at the base of this business relationship."

"Thanks, but it was mostly the lawyer." Callie smiled shyly, not used to being praised so much when it came to her work. She always just did it, and her commission was her praise.

"I doubt it," Hazel said with another wink before adding what they had to all be feeling, "Although I do wish Laurel were joining us."

Kenzie and Callie nodded as Saffron dropped her fork beside her plate.

"Don't you think it's a little strange that she opted out?" Saffron asked as she leaned back in her seat, and Callie nodded again. She had been thinking that. Laurel had not only agreed with them when they were eighteen that this was a good idea, but she often brought it up when they all got together in the times since. Callie knew Laurel was always busy with organizing charity events at the country club she and her husband belonged to on top of being a mom, but Callie didn't think she was too busy to join her friends in this, especially now that all of her children had flown the coop. And Callie knew the buy in wasn't a problem. Laurel's husband was a highly successful financial guru. Basically half of the town had invested money with him. Callie would have as well if her own father wasn't a retired financial planner. He gave her enough tips, and Callie liked investing on her own. But Laurel couldn't be hurting for money. Her husband loved to buy her lavish presents: diamonds, luxury cars, purses—you name it, the man had gifted it to Laurel. So Callie knew he'd be more than happy to hand over the money.

"I do. Did she give you any kind of an explanation, Callie?" Kenzie asked.

Callie shook her head. "Just what I told you girls. That this wasn't the best time."

"I wonder what that means?" Saffron asked, frowning, and Callie realized they really did need more of an answer. She didn't want to make Laurel feel bad about not joining them, but their friend's absence would be a dark cloud over the venture until they knew why she didn't want to do this.

Callie pushed her plate away, no longer hungry. She should be thrilled that she was buying this lodge with any of her friends, much less three of them. But that almost made it worse. If it had just been Callie and Saffron, the absence of Laurel wouldn't have felt so profound.

"Are you not going to finish that?" Hazel asked, and Callie shook her head as she passed her half-full plate down to Hazel.

"How are you able to keep enough food in the house for you and your teenaged boys?" Kenzie asked as she watched Hazel consume Callie's leftovers.

"It's expensive, that's for sure," Hazel said between bites, making Kenzie laugh.

Callie looked over at Saffron to see she was deep in thought. Probably about Laurel.

Just as she was about to move the conversation along—it wouldn't do to have them all moping—Callie swore she heard a familiar voice. Sure enough, when she looked across the restaurant, there stood Laurel, as if their thoughts had conjured her. Probably waiting for her to-go order, since she hadn't gone any further than the hostess desk. Laurel noticed them at the same moment Callie saw her because she watched as Laurel's eyes went wide with shock.

Callie stood, but Laurel waved, signaling she was coming to them.

Callie's movement caused the other three women at the table to turn and see Laurel headed their way. Hazel squealed in delight as she jumped up and ran to meet their friend in the middle of the restaurant, hugging her before letting go and looping their arms together to lead Laurel to their table.

Callie grinned as she noticed the height disparity between the two friends. Hazel was the tallest of their group at nearly five foot ten, and then there was cute, petite Laurel coming in at a whopping five feet nothing. Laurel had always hated her tiny frame in high school, but she had become more accepting of it over the years.

"Laurel," Kenzie said as she jumped up to hug their missing friend. Callie had to admit the entire atmosphere of their gathering shifted with Laurel's appearance. It was as if the hole they'd all been feeling was now full.

"We're so glad to see you, but what are you doing here?" Saffron asked as Laurel pointed back to the hostess desk.

"Just grabbing some lunch for Bennie and his associates," Laurel said.

"Is that why you aren't doing this with us?" Hazel asked, getting right to the heart of the matter. Hazel never beat around the bush.

"Is what? Oh, do you mean am I not joining you all on your venture because of Bennie's business obligations?" Laurel asked, her face morphing from confusion to a smile.

Hazel nodded. "Is he keeping you under his thumb? Because I could have a few words with him...."

Laurel raised her hands in defense of her husband. "Nothing like that," she assured them.

"Then why?" Callie asked, feeling the need for them to all know the truth behind Laurel's choice. Although they respected it, Callie was pretty sure they all felt as disappointed by Laurel's decision as Callie did.

"The timing," Laurel said again, and it sounded even more like a hollow excuse this time. There was something she wasn't saying. Something important.

"You wouldn't have to do anything for a couple of weeks. This beginning portion is all up to Callie," Saffron pointed out. They would all be dividing the work into their areas of expertise when the lodge finally opened, but before that the work would probably be a bit uneven as Callie would need to do more during the sale and Hazel would need to be more involved in the redecoration process.

"I know. But the timing won't be any better in a few weeks," Laurel said before she sighed. The sound was sad.

"Laurel, if there's anything..." Kenzie began, and Laurel shook her head.

"It's fine. We're fine," Laurel said with a fake smile if Callie had ever seen one. Laurel looked behind them to see that the hostess still didn't have her order ready. It was obvious she was looking for a way out of their conversation. But why? Laurel was one of them. They were always comfortable together. Except when they were keeping secrets. And it was obvious to Callie that Laurel was keeping a big secret.

"Laurel, it *isn't* fine, is it?" Callie prodded, and Laurel shook her head as her eyes welled with tears.

Callie immediately stood and gave her seat to Laurel as

Kenzie pulled up another chair for Callie from an empty table nearby.

"What is it?" Callie asked.

Hazel added, "If it's Bennie. I'll kill him. Or have him killed. Whatever you want."

That brought a bit of a strangled chuckle out of Laurel. "It is Bennie," she admitted, and Saffron's eyes went wide before she schooled her features. "But not in the way you think. He's in trouble. Well, we're in trouble." Laurel sighed again. "I promised him I'd say nothing, but the news will be out soon anyway. Bennie made some really bad investments."

Laurel swallowed and then looked around at the women who loved her. She must have seen what she needed on their faces because she continued in a whisper, "He's lost everything. His investors' money. Our money. All of it."

Callie couldn't help the small gasp that escaped her.

The sound seemed to knock Laurel out of her daze because she suddenly stood and looked around at the group as if she couldn't believe what she'd done. "Please don't..." She paused as if she was unsure of how to go on.

"We won't say a word," Kenzie promised as the other women quickly nodded in agreement. Laurel didn't even need to ask.

"Let us help you," Callie said as she turned in her chair to look up at Laurel.

CHAPTER FIVE

LAUREL COULD NOT BELIEVE she'd said anything. She'd promised Bennie she wouldn't. But it had been eating her up inside. The fact that she knew so many of her friends and neighbors would be finding out that all of their savings had been lost. Because of Bennie. Her other half. The only sigh of relief she could breathe was that none of the girls had invested with Bennie. Callie because she'd invested on her own, and the other three because they had their own financial advisors outside of Rosebud. Thank heaven for small miracles. But there weren't many in Laurel's circle that would escape the fallout. Even her own parents had invested a sizeable part of their retirement with Bennie. They still had a good amount of savings, but neither of them worked anymore, and Laurel didn't want to think what this news would mean for them. And she'd had to keep it all bottled up inside. Because Bennie said it would be best.

Although part of her felt a small respite being able to say the words aloud, the shame soon followed. How could this have happened? Her financial genius husband had lost it all. He had spent the last few weeks trying to make up for it, but nothing could be done, according to him. Laurel still wasn't sure what kind of risky investments he'd made for the money to be all gone like that. But she believed him when he said it was. He wouldn't be so distraught otherwise.

"I can't," Laurel said, finally responding to the words Callie had spoken. She knew her friends would want to help. They would feel obligated. But Laurel would be fine. Bennie would figure a way out of this. He always did.

"You can't or you won't?" Hazel asked, and Laurel wasn't sure how to answer her question. Maybe a bit of both.

"You need the lodge more than any of us do right now. The timing is perfect," Saffron said, but Laurel couldn't disagree more. She had absolutely nothing to offer. No skills, no work experience. At least before, she would have had money, but now? She truly had nothing. And it was all her fault for not having worked her entire marriage. At least then she would have had some kind of talents to offer the group even if she still would have had no money. Because even if she'd been making a good income, Bennie would have probably invested all that Laurel had made as well.

Laurel's mind strayed to her children, the reason why she hadn't worked for the first twenty years of her marriage to Bennie. Those years with twins and her little girl just a year younger had been busy ones. Thankfully, all three of them were grown, living in the city with good jobs of their own. Bennie had let her know that he had yet to invest any of their kids' money, so they wouldn't be harmed by this. At least not in the way she and Bennie would.

"Is it about the money?" Kenzie asked. Dear, sweet Kenzie would see the crux of the matter.

"That...and more," Laurel said before the entire group went quiet. The hostess was headed their way with two large bags of food. Laurel had asked her husband if ordering so much food was wise, considering they had no money, but Bennie had let her know keeping up appearances was important. So they had to do so until news broke.

"Here's your order, Mrs. Stockton," the hostess said, leaving the bags on the table in front of Laurel.

"Thank you, Jen," Laurel said to the hostess whose mom had invested with Bennie. Was there anyone in this town who wouldn't be affected by her husband's mismanagement?

Laurel looked in her wallet and gave all of her available cash to Jen as a tip.

Jen looked down at the three twenties, her mouth open.

"You already paid for the food earlier," Jen said, and Laurel nodded.

"I know. That's for you," Laurel said knowing Bennie wouldn't be happy with her decision. But that's what it had been. *Her* decision. She would live with the consequences.

"Thank you," Jen said as she hurried back to her station. Laurel knew Jen was taking a semester off from college in order to save up for the next year. What would happen when her mom found out about the loss of her investment? Would Jen have to leave school for even longer?

"I see those wheels turning. Tell us what's going on in there," Callie said softly.

Laurel wasn't sure what it was about Callie, but the woman had always been able to pull every secret from her. Even when Laurel had had her first kiss, something she had wanted to keep to herself because she had been the first of her friends to receive one. Callie had asked her about her date, and Laurel had spilled and told all four of them about that icky good night kiss.

"It's just...a lot. Everyone has invested in Bennie," Laurel said as tears began to fill her eyes again. She had to hold it together.

"And you're losing everything," Hazel added, and Laurel nodded.

"I could live with that a whole lot easier than the rest. Like Jen's mom—she invested. Now Jen, her siblings, and her mom will all be affected. Or more like infected. It truly feels like Bennie's actions are going to afflict everyone. Allen has invested. What if he loses the restaurant?" Laurel said as she watched the owner of the restaurant go to the hostess desk and then back to the kitchen.

"And the Mathesons sitting over there," Laurel said, her chest filling with panic, leaving it hard for her to breathe.

"Take a deep breath, Laurel," Callie commanded, and Laurel did.

"It will all work out. You just need to give it time," Hazel said as she rubbed Laurel's back.

Time. Right. Time until this all came out. Time until Bennie could make it better. Because he would. He had to. Time. She could give this all some time, couldn't she? She continued taking deep breaths, since they seemed to be working.

"Although we don't have time when it comes to the lodge. So until you can add in your share, I can give you the money," Kenzie offered, and Laurel coughed, nearly choking on one of her deep breaths. Because with those words, reality hit. Maybe time would make this better, but until then, she and Bennie would be some of the most hated people in town.

"I can't let you do that. I can't do that to any of you. When this gets out, and it will, I will be a pariah. And I deserve it. Anything I touch will turn to dust. I can't let the lodge be in the vicinity of the terror," Laurel said.

"Vicinity of the terror?" Saffron asked as Hazel chuckled.

"Okay, a little dramatic," Laurel admitted, but that was what she was feeling, and those words were the only ones that conveyed how deeply she was sure the fallout would go.

"The lodge will be fine," Kenzie assured her before saying, "We're more worried about you."

"I'll be fine. Bennie will figure it out the way he always does, and then we'll come stay at the lodge. Give you all some business," Laurel said, knowing she was being way too optimistic. But she did trust in her husband. He'd made this mistake, so he would correct it. He always had before, although his other mistakes had never been this large, but she had faith he'd somehow do what he always did. Make things right.

"Laurel, this won't be the same without you," Callie said softly, and all the women looked to her. "As much as Kenzie is saying you need something like the lodge right now, the lodge needs you. We need you."

Laurel shook her head. She doubted that.

"No, she's right," Hazel agreed. "This table felt empty without you. It's all or nothing, Laurel. It always has been, and it always should be."

"But the town is going to hate me," Laurel reminded them, and Saffron nodded.

"Probably, for a time. But we cater to tourists. They won't even know who you are," Saffron said as if it were the most logical thing in the world. And maybe it was. But backlash from the town wouldn't help them on their new venture.

"Besides, we will stand by your side whether you do this with us or not. If the town will hate us and the lodge because you're a part of the venture, they'll hate us just as much anyway because we are going to have your back through every step of this," Saffron added, and the other three women nodded in agreement.

Laurel shook her head. "No, that's why I said I couldn't do this. You all need to focus on the lodge, on your dreams, and let this all play out. You're right. It will blow over eventually, and then we'll see from there. But for now, keep me at arm's length. Let people know you didn't want me to be a part of the venture."

"Never," Hazel and Kenzie said in unison.

"You must have lost your dang mind if you think we'd do that to you," Saffron added.

"We aren't taking no for an answer, Laurel," Callie said, and Laurel turned her head to each of those sitting around that table. They couldn't all agree with Callie, could they? But as she looked to Saffron, then Hazel, and finally Kenzie, they all looked as determined as Callie.

"I know the buy-in is an issue. But I'll write up a contract to get around that. You'll be an employee of the lodge with an option to buy in later. That way you won't be getting any charity. You'd be in this because we need you," Callie said, and Laurel shook her head. She, unlike the rest of them, had no specialty to offer. There was no way they needed her.

"What could I do?" Laurel asked.

"You'd be the events coordinator," Callie said as if it was pure logic that they give that task to Laurel. Anyone could put together a meet and greet, plan a party. That didn't take any type of talent.

"You have years of experience," Kenzie said, probably meaning the charity work Laurel had done. But that wasn't the same.

"I have no *professional* experience," Laurel responded.

"Just because you weren't paid doesn't mean the experience isn't professional. Those events you put on were the talk of the town. The neighboring towns too," Callie said, and Laurel frowned.

"This isn't a good idea," Laurel said.

"It's the *best* idea," Kenzie said with a smile.

Callie added, "It's the only idea. Hazel was right. This is all or nothing."

Laurel looked to each of her friends and knew none of them would back down. And she wanted to say yes. Having to say no to Callie when she'd asked about the lodge had only compounded her deep sadness at what was happening in her life.

"There has to be a contingency in the contract," Laurel said, using her last shred of energy in standing up to her friends. Because she was tired of holding them at arm's length, but she had to do this. "If you all regret this..."

"We won't," Saffron interjected.

"If you do, there has to be a clause that lets you fire me. If anyone wants to, at any time," Laurel stated firmly.

"That's a bit over the top. You know Hazel will be getting upset with all of us all the time," Kenzie said with a grin, and Hazel glared at her friend before nodding in agreement.

"She does have a point," Hazel said. "Soften that language."

"Nope. It's the only way I'll feel okay about doing this. If the pressure of my life gets to be too much for anyone, especially the business, I'm out," Laurel reiterated, and Callie met her eyes.

Laurel hoped she looked as determined as she felt.

"Fine," Callie said with a single nod. "But it can't just be one of us. It doesn't have to be a majority, but it has to at least be two. And we aren't backing down on that."

Laurel looked to each of her friends, knowing them too well. She knew they wouldn't give in. And deep down she really wanted to join them in this venture.

So she did.

"Then I guess we're all in."

And she let her friends whoop and holler, pulling Allen out of the kitchen to see what the commotion was about. And just for this moment, Laurel let herself revel in that wonderful feeling. Because she knew there were a whole lot of bad days coming.

CHAPTER SIX

"THEY REJECTED THE OFFER," Callie's assistant said, poking her head into Callie's office.

"They rejected what?" Callie asked. For most, rejection wasn't a pleasant thing, and it really wasn't for Callie either, but it was a part of everyday life for a real estate agent. So it was something she'd grown accustomed to.

"The offer on the lodge," Sydney said, stepping into the office.

"Say what?" Callie asked, turning so that her ear was toward Sydney. She must have misheard.

"Clement just emailed," Sydney replied cautiously. The whole office knew how much this one offer meant to Callie.

"He emailed *you?*" Callie repeated. She couldn't understand it. The offer was basically a done deal. She had a relationship with Clement, a working one, but still. It was a good one. They'd been friends—well, as close to friends as competitors could be—for years now. Callie had been thrilled when the sellers of the lodge had gone with Clement as their agent. The only thing better would have been if the family who owned the lodge had come straight to her.

But the relationship she had with Clement was owed more than an email when the sellers were *rejecting* the offer. The amazing offer that had taken Callie weeks to draw up so it would be just perfect, especially when she knew for a fact that the sellers had no other offers on the table. Clement had told her that much.

"Yeah," Sydney said as she scrunched up her nose, a sure sign that she was uncomfortable. But Callie couldn't worry about that. She needed more information.

"You mean they sent a counter, right?" Callie asked. A counter offer would make more sense. It would still be annoying, since Clement had told Callie all she needed to do was write up her best offer and then he'd sell it to his clients, but still. A counter she could work with. She wasn't sure her friends would want to pony up more cash, but Callie would be willing to do it if no one else would. She wouldn't let go of this dream.

Sydney shook her head. "They rejected the offer," she reiterated. "Something about the terms being unacceptable?"

"Forward me that email. And then get Clement on the phone. An *email*," Callie muttered the last two words under her breath.

Sydney was nothing if not efficient, and by the time Callie opened up her email a few minutes later, there was the forwarded email from Clement. She made a note to give Sydney a large Christmas bonus.

Sure enough, the offer had been rejected. And sure enough, Callie was given no other information than the terms were unacceptable. What terms? Everything she'd included in the offer was typical of any real estate transaction. In fact, Callie might have been too eager and given the sellers a better deal than they deserved. Well, no more. She was ready to play hardball.

At that moment, Callie's phone rang, and she picked up immediately.

"I have Mr. Clement on the line for you?" Sydney said, and Callie sat up straighter, getting her mind and body ready for battle.

"Put him through," Callie said, her voice cool and collected. One thing she'd learned over the years of being in a business largely ruled by men: there was no place for emotions in the workplace. Well, at least no female emotions. She'd seen other agents, all male, throw fits and temper tantrums when they hadn't gotten their way. But it was never like that for Callie. She couldn't allow it. Because, whereas those men were quickly forgiven, behavior like that would have earned Callie a reputation as an unmanageable woman. It was unfair and totally sexist, but the way the world worked. For now, at least. Callie hoped things would be better for future generations.

"Mr. Clement," Callie said, using the same professional manner Sydney had even though what Callie wanted to do was rip this guy a new one. He'd made promises...and then tore them all away.

"Callie, it's good to hear from you," Clement said, and it was easy to hear the lie in his shaky voice. Good. He *should* be nervous.

"How is your wife?" Callie asked, knowing Clement would hate the pleasantries. He liked to get right into business, but Callie wasn't playing by his terms.

"Good, good," Clement answered quickly.

"And the kids? I heard Bobby will be joining your office next month? How did time fly by so fast? I swear we were just watching him play Little League," Callie said as a reminder to Clement that they were friends. Longtime friends. And she deserved better than the treatment she was getting.

"I couldn't go against what my client wanted," Clement said, clearly over the guilt trip Callie was laying. But she wasn't quite done yet.

"And did Marie get the gift I sent her? That baby of hers is incredibly adorable," Callie continued as if Clement had said nothing.

"Callie, I get it. We're friends. But my client saw your offer and couldn't accept," Clement said.

"They didn't even want to give us a counter?" Callie asked.

"She—I mean *they* were adamant," Clement said, but Callie didn't miss his slip.

She. Callie ran through her mental catalog of the McPhersons, the family who was selling the lodge. The grandparents had been the last generation who'd loved the place and cared for it the way Callie and her friends would. But they had since passed on, and the lodge had gone to the next generation, the ones about Callie's age, who were now in charge of the place. They had attempted for a few years to put in minimal effort and hoped for maximum profit. But now that they could no longer get a great profit, thanks to the years of neglect, they were selling. There was also a younger generation, the kids. And though they would probably get a bit of the money from the sale after it went through, Callie was almost positive they would have no say in the actual sales transaction. So it was just the women Callie's age who could have vetoed the sale.

But that didn't give Callie much, considering there were two brothers and their wives and then two sisters along with their respective husbands. So she'd narrowed down the opposition to four possible people, but that was still too many to figure out what was going on. However, luckily for her, she was on the phone with the one person who knew exactly which of those four possible people had the complaint.

"Who, Clement?" Callie asked, and she heard shuffling on the other side of the phone. She knew Clement was shaking his head.

"You know better than anyone the kind of trouble we can get into for sharing information like that," Clement said.

Callie fought her frown. She wasn't giving in.

"You don't have to give me a reason. Just a name would suffice," she added, but the rustling continued.

Okay, she'd have to come up with a different tactic.

"If they didn't give us a counter, that either means we offended them with our offer..." Callie waited to see if there was a reaction on the other end of the line. Nothing.

Okay, she was pretty sure that meant that the sellers weren't offended by the offer. And that would be what made sense. There was absolutely nothing offensive about the offer. So there was only one other conclusion.

"Or it's personal," Callie said, and Clement cleared his throat.

So it *was* personal. Callie had thought that instead of staying anonymous, it would help if she and her friends wrote letters about why the lodge meant so much to them, and she'd send those in with her offer. But it looked like that idea may have backfired. Shoot.

Callie began to run through possible negative personal connections she could have had with the family, but she couldn't find any. The generation at the negotiation table were homegrown, so she knew quite a bit about each of them. But she had no particular relationship with any of them. Not that she knew of at least. It could get kind of messy living in a small town for all of one's life. Callie could have stolen a parking spot or something silly like that which could have had someone holding a grudge, but she doubted it. Because she worked in this town and had grown her business in this town, she knew the goings on pretty well. She'd gone to events the McPherson sisters had also attended, and they'd all had a marvelous time. The sisters-in-law weren't as social as the sisters, at least in Callie's circles, but she'd waved at them at the grocery store and the mall. And they always waved back. So she really doubted they hated her. That meant it was one of her four friends.

"Please tell me who," Callie practically begged, but Clement stayed silent. She should have known he wouldn't budge. Friendship or not, he was keeping his commitment to his clients. Something Callie would have admired...had this offer not meant so much to her.

"You promised me, Clement," Callie knew she was walking on thin ice. She was making this personal; granted, the sellers had done that first, but then again, she was the professional here. But she had to make Clement relent. At least a little more.

"I know, Callie. And I feel horrible. I had no idea the sellers would have this kind of an issue. Your offer was good. It should have been accepted," Clement said, and Callie knew he meant every word. But she also knew there was nothing else he would do. *Could* do.

"I could speak to the sellers myself," Callie said, and Clement grunted.

"I wish you luck with that. Getting that group together is about as easy as wrangling kittens," Clement said jovially, but Callie couldn't even smile.

What recourse did she have? There had to be something more she could do.

"We could offer more money," Callie said.

"They wouldn't accept it," Clement replied immediately.

Whatever the hurt was, it ran deep.

"And, Callie?" Clement added. "This stays between us. I am only telling you because of our friendship. But they have another offer coming."

"What?" Callie gasped. She'd heard nothing about any other interest in the lodge. And she had a pretty good hand on the pulse of this town.

"Out-of-towners," Clement said, and Callie closed her eyes. Of course. She should have known the big guns would be coming in. This lodge, her lodge, was on prime wine country real estate. Not only was the actual building beautiful, the land was worth a whole lot. Especially if a developer came in and divided it up into multiple lots. But did zoning allow for that? Callie was about to look it up when she realized it didn't matter. If another offer was coming in, they had a plan. And they would surely know what the zoning was for the property if they planned on splitting it up.

"I'm expecting an offer by the end of next week," Clement added.

Ten days. That was all Callie had to figure out what was wrong and somehow make it right.

"Clement, you don't want some big developer to come and put in a few mini mansions, do you?" Callie asked. As much as they both loved their jobs, Callie and Clement were in the same camp when it came to overdeveloping certain parts of their town. Sure, Callie had bought a tract of land a few years back and done the same thing these moguls were planning on doing. But the tract she'd bought wasn't the lodge. She didn't tear down a building that was part of the heart of their town.

"Talk to Hazel," was all Clement said before hanging up.

Hazel?

"ARE you sure you want to go on your own?" Hazel asked as Sterling held his skateboard flush against his body.

The therapist's office wasn't far, but it was Sterling's first time going to this woman and Hazel wanted to check her out. Dr. April Brand hadn't grown up in Rosebud, so Hazel knew nothing about her. Well, other than the word on the street, which was that this doctor was practically a miracle worker. But still, Hazel wanted to see that for herself before letting her baby boy have a therapy visit with her. If she had known Sterling was going to be so adamant about going on his own, she would have scheduled her own appointment with the doctor first. But when the receptionist had told Hazel there was one free appointment this week and two next week, it seemed like a no brainer to send Sterling, who would soon be needing a refill of his meds. Now she was rethinking that position. What if Dr. Brand was just a charmer? And she had the whole town fooled? And what if she also worked her magic on Sterling? Bad magic, not good magic.

Hazel knew that her imagination was running away with her, but she couldn't help it. It was now solely up to her to protect her boys. And she would. Even from perfectly harmless therapists.

"Mom, I'll be fine. You filled out all of the paperwork online, and it isn't like this is my first time going to a shrink," Sterling said, and Hazel raised a warning eyebrow.

She hated it when the boys used the word *shrink* instead of *therapist*. It demeaned not only the doctor they were seeing but the process her boys were going through. They needed the help they were getting, and calling the therapist a shrink seemed to minimize what the person could do. Maybe it didn't make sense, but Hazel held strong on that rule.

"It isn't your first time to a therapist, but it's your first time to this one," Hazel responded as Sterling blew his long bangs out of his eyes. What was with her boys and hating haircuts?

"I've been to, like, a hundred appointments that will be just like this one. I'll be fine, Mom," Sterling said as he dropped his skateboard to the ground and then rolled toward the door.

Sterling hadn't been to quite a hundred therapy sessions, but he had experienced his fair share. And he was right. He'd be fine on his own. It was Hazel who was having the problems.

"No boarding in the house," Hazel called as he left. Obligingly, Sterling kicked up his board and walked the remainder of the way to the front door.

Sterling wasn't quite the skater that his brother was—he just didn't have the passion for it—but he'd learned enough to get around because he had a passion for independence.

Hazel heard the front door open and then Sterling say, "Oh, hey, Aunt Callie."

Although neither of her boys knew her high school friends well, when Callie had been reacquainted with the boys the week before, she'd insisted they both call her Aunt Callie the way that Laurel's kids did. Hazel loved that. Because she and her girls were like family. Sure, they'd been apart for some years, but they'd come back together. The way she'd always known they would. Families, careers, and lifestyles had kept them physically apart, but her friends were a part of who Hazel was. And those kinds of people automatically became family.

"Hello Sterling. Is your mom around?" Hazel heard Callie ask.

"She's in her lair," Sterling said, and Hazel rolled her eyes.

She still hadn't decided what to call the room she sat in because technically it was a formal dining room. But calling it an office felt weird, since it didn't even have a door, she used a dining table as her workspace, and really there was nothing else in the room. As of yet. She had some decorating plans. But she was in the process of procuring the right pieces. In the meantime, her boys had taken to calling the room her lair. Like she was an evil villain.

Boys.

"Your lair, huh?" Callie asked as she entered the room. She looked around, probably expecting a lot more, considering Hazel's decorating reputation on social media and beyond.

"Don't worry, I'll decorate the lodge in a much better way

than this," Hazel promised. She already had dozens of sketches for what she wanted to do with the magnificent space that would soon be theirs. This one space was just harder than most because it was so personal. But Hazel had no difficulty decorating others' homes or even the common areas of her own.

"I'm not worried," Callie said before adding, "Well, at least about that."

Hazel waved to the chair beside her, and Callie took a seat.

Callie continued to look around the room, and Hazel wondered what she saw. The room was pretty with its molding and gaudy chandelier. Hazel loved a good gaudy chandelier. And the room was bright, thanks to its position at the corner of the house. Two gigantic windows on two walls let in enormous amounts of daylight.

But then Hazel really looked at her friend and saw that her eyes were glazed over. She wasn't really looking at the room. She was hesitating. And Hazel didn't like that. Callie didn't hesitate. Whatever brought her here couldn't be good news.

"Do you remember the McPhersons?" Callie asked, and Hazel nodded.

Most of the lifelong residents of the town knew one another. Sure, Hazel had left for about thirty years, but she felt she was still in the know thanks to her friends and her parents still living in town.

"They own the lodge," Hazel said.

Callie gnawed on her lip, her long pause causing Hazel to hold her breath.

"How well do you know them?" Callie asked, and Hazel let out her breath to speak.

"Get to the point, Cal," Hazel prodded, and Callie nodded.

"Someone in the family rejected our offer because of you," Callie said, meeting Hazel's eyes. The words were said matter-of-factly, so they didn't hurt. At least until Hazel really thought about it.

"They rejected our offer?" Hazel asked, and Callie nodded again.

"You mean they gave us a counter that is too terrible to consider, right?" Hazel continued.

Callie shook her head. "I wish. That would be better than what we got. Nothing."

Hazel put her elbows on the table and then her chin in her hands. "And it's because of me?"

"Clement didn't tell me much, but he did say *she* rejected the offer and that I should speak to you."

"But I don't know anything," Hazel groaned as her head dropped so her hands were at her temples. "The sisters love me. We used to cheer together back in high school."

Recollection brightened in Callie's eyes. "I forgot they both cheered," she said, and Hazel nodded.

"Well, what about the sisters-in-law?" Callie asked.

"The who?" Hazel responded. She should probably have realized that the McPherson boys would have married, but it was weird when one didn't see people since high school. They just stayed those annoying boys who were a few years older than she was. And since Hazel never went on social media for personal reasons, she'd had no way of casually seeing that kind of news.

"Mike and Jim. They married Sue and Rachel," Callie responded, and Hazel felt her gut fall.

No, it had to be another Sue, right? They went to high school with, like, four Sue's. Or the boys could have married women who hadn't grown up in Rosebud. But even before Callie said anything, Hazel knew it had to be Sue Morton. Who else would have a vendetta against Hazel? Who else would be blocking their offer?

"That wouldn't by any chance be Sue Morton who married a McPherson, would it?" Hazel asked cautiously.

Callie frowned. "What did you do to Sue Morton?" she asked and then corrected, "McPherson."

"Do you remember Dylan Pinnegar?" Hazel asked, thinking back to the boy she'd dated for a hot minute back in eleventh grade. He had been beautiful. But he'd also been bad news. And he was always on again and off again with his very longtime girlfriend, Sue Morton.

"No," Callie responded, and Hazel wasn't surprised. It wasn't like she'd publicized that relationship. She knew her friends would have talked her out of dating the guy, but he'd been so good looking and he was technically single. Well, at least according to him. Hazel later found out that, at least according to Sue, Dylan and Sue had still been together. Hazel had tried to apologize, but the girl wouldn't hear her out. Sue had started raging at Hazel, and Hazel, somewhat afraid for her well-being, had run away. That had been the end of it.

Or so she'd thought.

"This is all over a boy?" Callie asked.

"You have to remember Dylan," Hazel said, easily conjuring images of the all too handsome guy.

Callie narrowed her eyes, seeming to flick through a mental catalog. Then she gasped. "Of course, Dylan Pinnegar! He *was* beautiful. He moved out of town right after high school, didn't he?"

Hazel nodded. It had been soon after she and Dylan had dated, since he'd been a senior when Hazel had been a junior.

"Right, he was Sue's boyfriend all through...please tell me you didn't date him." Callie groaned as she dropped her face into her hands.

"It was for, like, a month. Maybe not even that long. He and Sue were on a break and..."

"And you had a crush on him. Yeah, I know how it goes when there's a boy you like. You had to take advantage of that time off," Callie said.

Hazel grimaced. She wasn't exactly proud of that aspect of her past.

"He told me they were done," she defended herself.

"You didn't believe him, did you?" Callie asked as if Hazel were still considering dating the guy.

"Of course I did," Hazel said and then amended, "well, I kind of did. Or maybe I hoped it was the truth?"

Callie nodded, obviously understanding that. "But is she really holding onto something from so long ago? A boy from high school?" she asked incredulously.

If she was, Hazel didn't exactly blame Sue. The girl—well, they were girls then—had been obsessed with Dylan. Even more than Hazel had been. And Hazel could still feel a tiny tug on her heart when it came to Dylan Pinnegar. Even though she was still mad as heck at him because he'd either lied to her or not told Sue firmly enough that they were over before he'd started dating Hazel. Either way, it had created this rift with Sue. Although, to be fair, there might still have been a rift with Sue even if they had been completely over and done when Hazel had entered the picture. Sue was that into Dylan. And if Hazel was honest with herself, she wouldn't have cared even if she had known that Sue thought she and Dylan were still together. Dylan Pinnegar had seemed a prize enough that any downsides were worth it. Oh, she'd been foolish at seventeen.

As she reminisced, suddenly Hazel remembered one last argument with Sue in the weeks after Dylan had left town. Sue had said Dylan left because of Hazel. Which Hazel had never understood. When she'd broken up with Dylan because she'd gotten sick of all the drama she had to deal with while dating him, he'd gone right back to Sue. And they'd been back together for months before Dylan had left town. But because Sue had blamed Hazel for his abandonment, Hazel decided it was worth telling Callie about that one last conversation with Sue.

"So she blames you for the love of her life leaving her. I guess I can see why we lost the lodge," Callie said bluntly when Hazel finished.

Hazel grimaced. When she put it like that? Hazel knew Callie was too nice to come right out and say it, but she was the reason they'd lost the lodge. So she needed to try to fix it.

"What do we do now?" Callie asked.

But Hazel had no idea how to answer. "Should I try to talk to her?" She didn't particularly want to do so, but she'd feel terrible if they all lost the lodge because of her.

Callie shook her head. "Normally, I would say yes, but considering how she reacted when she last spoke to you and the fact that she's nursing a thirty-year-old grudge against you, I'd say that's not a good idea."

Hazel had to agree.

"I could put in more money. What if we upped the offer?" Hazel asked, but Callie shook her head again.

"I tried that. Clement said no amount of money could sway her."

Hazel bit her lip. Man, the hate must run deep. And if it wasn't going to hurt their plans—and especially her friends—she honestly wouldn't care. Sure, she felt bad about what she'd done. But it had been high school. And she'd tried to apologize. If Sue still hated her, that was on Sue.

"I thought if we figured out what had gone wrong, we could fix it, but this seems unfixable," Callie moaned as she leaned against the back of her chair and slouched. Callie didn't slouc,h and it made Hazel uncomfortable to watch.

"Saffron has already started the process of selling her share of her restaurant. Kenzie needs this to keep her sane during

Bryan's health journey, and we all know this is probably Laurel's only saving grace right now," Callie continued, and Hazel was suddenly overwhelmed by frustration. The women were counting on this. Her best friends were counting on her.

She sat up straight in her chair. "I'll take care of this. I'll make the family see reason. I'll talk to Sue, and if that doesn't work, I'll talk to Mike if I have to."

"Sue married Jim," Callie corrected.

"Right, I'll talk to Jim."

"Hazel, I'm not sure...."

"I made the mess. Let me fix it," Hazel pleaded, and she saw the pity in Callie's eyes.

"It isn't your fault..." Callie tried, but Hazel cut her off.

"Except that it is."

"Let me see what I can do on my end. This is my career. And I'm good at my job. I've never come across a problem I couldn't solve in my work world," Callie said with renewed confidence as she stood.

"Except maybe that's the issue. This is the first time your professional life is crossing paths with your personal one," Hazel pointed out, but Callie shook her head.

"So I just make it impersonal. I take a step back. I solve this problem," Callie said resolutely, but for once in their life, Hazel wasn't sure if Callie's grit and elbow grease would be enough to solve the problem at hand.

"I don't know if that will work this time," Hazel said softly, hating that she was doubting Callie, but this was too close to home for professional Callie to see this through. And it was completely Hazel's fault things had gone south.

"I could always go to Jim and the others. They can't know Sue is blocking the deal because of a boy from high school and be okay with it, can they?" Callie worked through a plan aloud.

"What if Sue is ready with a lie? Another reason why she

wasn't willing to take the deal? It would make us look petty and be even worse in the long run, wouldn't it?" Hazel asked. "And they could already know the truth. Confronting them could cause them to dig their heels in, and then we'd have no means of salvation."

Callie nodded, knowing Hazel was right. She rubbed her temples as she thought. She opened her mouth to speak and then closed it again, going back to rubbing her temples.

"I think I really am out of options," Callie said with a groan. Hazel hated that she'd done this to her friend. Callie was always the one with a plan. But now, when it mattered most, her plans were failing. This had to be killing her.

"So let me make this right," Hazel asked again, and Callie met Hazel's eyes. Hazel could see from her friend's gaze that she wasn't sure Hazel was up to the task, but then she saw Callie sigh and Hazel knew she had her. That was Callie's *what do I have to lose* sigh.

"I'll talk to Sue. I'll talk to them. I'll grovel, beg, whatever it takes. And if that doesn't work, I'll make my ex put on a private concert for the family in exchange for an accepted offer. Although he's not a dream to live with, everyone is a Wells Harrington fan," Hazel promised, and Callie finally smiled.

"Now that sounds like a plan I can get behind," Callie said as she walked out of the room.

Thank goodness Callie felt that way. Because it had to work. Since groveling and offering her ex on a platter were the only plans Hazel had.

CHAPTER SEVEN

"ABSOLUTELY NOT," Garrett, Saffron's soon-to-be-ex business partner, said. Except, apparently, if it were up to Garrett, there would be no *ex*.

"What do you mean, absolutely not?" Saffron asked softly. They had taken one of the most private tables at their restaurant for their business meeting, but they were still right next to paying customers. Saffron wasn't about to make a scene.

"I mean absolutely not. We will not buy you out," Garrett said, and Sanders—their third business partner and Garrett's best friend—nodded. Because Sanders nodded to anything and everything Garrett said.

"*Why* not?" Saffron asked. She really hadn't seen this coming. The guys had been wary about letting Saffron buy in in the first place. They hadn't felt the need for a third partner. They had capital lined up, thanks to family oil money from Sanders, and both Sanders and Garrett were excellent chefs. Some of the best San Francisco had to offer. So Saffron had had to push to join them. She'd known the opportunity to work with these two would be incredible. There had already been so much buzz about the place. She knew she'd never have the money to start up a restaurant on her own, and she really didn't want to work with investors who knew lots about money but nothing about food. Besides, she actually liked Garrett and Sanders, which was high praise considering she disliked nearly half of the chefs in San Francisco. What was it with males who could cook being pompous jerks?

So they'd finally, after weeks of persuading, let Saffron in on the deal. But she had assumed that because they hadn't truly wanted her to be a part of this in the first place, they'd easily let her out of their agreement now.

"First off, we don't have the capital. At least in cash right now," Garrett said and then looked to Sanders, who nodded in agreement.

"What about the oil money that was going to cover my third before you let me buy in?" Saffron asked, and Sanders blushed as Garrett puffed out his chest.

"There wasn't actually any money. At least not to cover more than what we already put into the restaurant. We were going to find investors for the last third," Garrett said with no guilt, and Saffron felt her own face go red. But there was no shame behind her redness, just fury.

"You lied?!" she asked and then shushed herself, remembering where she was seated.

"It didn't seem smart to go into business with..." Sanders paused the very first sentence he'd uttered in the conversation, but Saffron could fill in the blank. *With a woman.*

"You hadn't really proved yourself..." Garrett began, but Saffron cut him off.

"I worked with Gustav for fifteen years," Saffron pointed out the relationship she'd had with the chef she knew they all revered.

"Yeah. But you were the token female in his kitchen. And

better yet, you were a woman of color," Garrett said, and Saffron felt her eyes go wide.

"Please tell me I misheard what you just said," Saffron said barely keeping control of the anger she felt.

"Saffron, you know how it goes. Feminists get mad when there isn't a single female in the kitchen, so chefs keep that one woman on their payroll," Garrett said as if he were spouting off facts instead of ridiculous opinions. "And you were Gustav's get-out-of-jail-free card. If anyone got mad at him, he'd point to you."

"You think I got my job with Gustav because I'm a woman?" Saffron didn't raise her voice, but it was easy to hear the knives behind her words.

"And because you're black," Garrett continued as if he had no care for his well-being. At least Sanders was beginning to lean away from his friend. Sanders had always been good about self-preservation.

"And a man would have had my job otherwise," Saffron said through gritted teeth.

"Obviously," Garrett said and then added, "but you've done a great job here. We're proud of your work."

As if those placating words could erase the ugly ones he'd just spewed.

But then again, what had Saffron done to disprove Garrett? Sure, she'd worked her butt off and she'd had no idea that his opinion of her was so low, but she'd allowed him and Sanders to mistreat her day after day. To keep her working day in and day out while they put in appearances. She had made all of the hard decisions, and they'd basked in the glory of the praise the restaurant received. She'd let them use her poorly. She'd let them give so little and get so much in return. She hadn't made them appreciate her worth. And now it was so much worse than she'd thought. She'd assumed they were friends, but now she knew better.

"So what made you change your mind about me and decide to let me invest? Because that was before you saw my *great* work here," Saffron asked, not able to help the sarcasm that crept into her voice.

Garrett turned to Sanders. "You had the money, and Sanders reminded me we could have our very own token female," Garrett replied, and at least Sanders had the decency not to agree with that statement, but Saffron was done.

She had hoped she could have an amicable conversation with two men she'd respected. That the three friends could find the best way to dissolve this professional relationship, but she'd been wrong.

Saffron stood and looked down at the men she'd once admired. Who she thought had had her back.

"You'll be hearing from my lawyer," Saffron said as she turned to walk away.

"Don't do this, Saffron," she heard Sanders ask quietly.

"You'll regret it," Garrett added, and those words got Saffron moving faster, anger fueling her every step. She had nothing more to say.

SAFFRON NERVOUSLY SLAPPED the manila folder containing the contract she'd signed with her ex business partners against her thigh as she walked from where she'd parked her car to her attorney's office. She'd thought about going with a big city lawyer the way she knew Garrett and Sanders would, but realized that wasn't her style. And not only that, Rosebud's resident civil attorney was a hidden gem. Riley Matthews had graduated at the top of his class from UC-Berkley, one of the top law schools in the nation, and then had come home, creaming the competition on the local legal scene. Not only would Riley bring a case to court that would rival, if not outshine, her ex business partners' case, he was a friend. A real one, unlike Garrett and Sanders had been.

Saffron had already sent an electronic version of the contract to Riley, but she wanted to bring in the paper copy as well. Mostly for her peace of mind, but also Riley had said it would be nice to see the original.

"Saffron," Hazel nearly shouted from where she stood right next to Saffron, causing her to jump.

"Why are you yelling?" Saffron reprimanded her friend.

"I've been calling your name for the last minute. I ran all the way from Velma's, calling your name the entire time, and you didn't hear me until I was right here," Hazel said through her laughter, and Saffron would have joined her had she not been so nervous.

"What's up?" Hazel asked as she took in Saffron's nervous tapping of the manila folder as well as her pale face.

"I'm meeting with Riley," Saffron said, and Hazel nodded, her face filling with understanding.

All of Saffron's friends were aware of how her meeting with Garrett and Sanders had gone. And they all knew Saffron was going to hire their high school classmate, Riley. Hazel's response to the text thread had been, *Sink your teeth into them, Saff!*

"Do you want me to come with you?" Hazel offered, and Saffron shook her head even though she really wanted to say yes. Having the comfort of a best friend by her side after having felt so alone and betrayed by Garrett and Sanders would have been incredible. But she was a big girl. She could and should do this on her own. Besides, Hazel had to have better things to do.

Saffron gave Hazel her second excuse, and Hazel scoffed.

"I did just tell you I came from Velma's. Saff, I'm at a bakery in the middle of the day, and did you notice I came out with no purchases? I'm trying to cut back on the sweets but am failing miserably. I was about to eat my third candy bar of the day but barely stopped myself. As a way to keep myself strong, I went into Velma's just to sniff her sweet air. You'd be saving me from my sweet tooth if you let me go to this meeting with you. Besides, I might be of some help. You may have noticed I made out like a bandit after my divorce. I could do the same for you," Hazel said with a pump of her eyebrows, and Saffron finally smiled.

"See, I'm good for you already," Hazel said as she nudged Saffron's arm with her shoulder.

"Fine," Saffron said and then realized how ungrateful she sounded. "And thank you," she added, and Hazel waved the words away.

"What are sisters for?"

Saffron fought the emotion that welled within her chest. Sisters. This was who she was getting into business with this time. Getting out of the restaurant and joining the girls to open the lodge was the best decision she could have ever made.

Hazel looped an arm through Saffron's, and they made their way into the mighty cold offices of Riley Matthews, Esquire.

Saffron checked in with the receptionist, who promised Mr. Matthews would be right out, before taking a seat next to Hazel.

"Do you think he's trying to keep an igloo frozen somewhere back there?" Hazel asked while rubbing her arms up and down.

"Or maybe a penguin habitat?" Saffron offered, and Hazel grinned.

"I like your option much better. Although don't you think we would have smelled a penguin habitat?" Hazel asked.

"You're right," Saffron said. "It's definitely an igloo."

"An igloo?" Riley asked as he joined them in the waiting room.

Saffron felt her cheeks go red at being caught in such a ridiculous conversation. Riley was a friend, but she'd hoped to start their meeting on a more professional foot. She had no idea how to explain what she'd said without coming off as having a couple of screws loose.

"We were just debating why you keep your office so cold," Hazel supplied, and Saffron shot a smile at her friend. "I decided you must be trying to keep an igloo frozen." Thank goodness Hazel always kept her wits about her. She made the whole thing sound like the joke it was, and her explanation had been just enough that neither of them ended up seeming nutty.

"Nope. I wish it was something as interesting as that. But alas, the coldness is just representative of the heart that beats in my chest. All those rumors you've heard about lawyers? They're all true," Riley said with a grin, causing Hazel and Saffron to laugh.

Saffron was impressed by the way Riley didn't seem intimidated by Hazel the way he would have been back in the day. Granted, it had been many years since high school, but she'd seen quite a few of their male former classmates get tongue tied whenever Hazel was around.

But then again, Riley had been Saffron's friend in high school, and even though Saffron and Hazel had been friends, Riley hadn't hung out anywhere near the sphere of Hazel and her cheer friends. The young teen he was would never have been able to crack a joke in front of the most beautiful girl at Rosebud High. But it looked like the National Honor Society's president had found some humor and backbone in the thirty years since high school, and the youthful look that had worked against him back then was sure working for him now. Not that Saffron would ever be interested romantically in Riley Matthews, hot or not. But she noticed Hazel grinning up at the man's dark hair and matching dark eyes, and it looked like maybe Hazel could be interested?

"So I went over your contract," Riley said as he guided the women toward his office, tugging off his coat and showing off his broad shoulders. Saffron tried not to smile as she glanced over at Hazel, who appeared to be trying not to drool at the sight.

Riley offered them each a seat in his office and then sat across from them in a chair instead of behind his huge, dark wood desk. Diplomas and awards hung on his walls, along with a few pictures of the beach just an hour west of Rosebud. A window sat behind Riley's office chair, and there were two large bookcases framing the window and filled with gigantic books that looked like they must weigh at least as much as a small child.

The office would intimidate most people, but to Saffron, something about Riley's affable manner made it welcoming.

"And?" Saffron asked as she handed Riley the manila envelope with her paper copy.

"Did you have an attorney write that up for you?" Riley asked, and Saffron shook her head. They hadn't seen the need. They each knew what they wanted out of the restaurant, and they'd made sure to include that in the contract. Saffron had taken Callie with her to the final signing, and that had felt like enough, considering all of Callie's experience with contracts. Although Saffron guessed Callie had never seen a contract like the one she and her partners had drawn up.

"I assumed as much. You have nearly nothing about what would happen when someone wants to dissolve this partnership," Riley said, and Saffron frowned.

"Is that bad?" Saffron asked.

"It could be. If you didn't have such an excellent attorney now," Riley said with a smile that put Saffron at ease. She had been right to hire him.

"You each put in a third of the startup costs, is that correct?" Riley asked, and Saffron nodded. None of the three of them were business people, but they had figured that as long as they put in the same amount of money and the restaurant worked out, who cared about the rest? The only thing the contract had been sure to state was what would happen if the restaurant didn't see success. Whenever the majority decided it was time to get out, they would. Saffron could now see that the men had worded it that way so they could always use their vote to bully Saffron. How had she not seen it before?

"And then we took out a loan to cover everything else we needed," Saffron said, again feeling foolish. She hadn't even asked why they weren't using the supposed oil money Sanders had instead of getting a loan. She'd just assumed it was so that they could keep things fair and because the men didn't want her to feel bad that she couldn't contribute more monetarily. Little did she know...but dwelling on all of that now would not help her. She needed to focus on Riley. The man who was going to help her out of this.

"We paid back the loan within five years, and we've been profitable ever since," Saffron said. That statement filled her with pride, pushing away the uncertainty she had started to feel any time she thought about the partnership she was trying to dissolve. The wild success of the restaurant was one thing she had no reason to feel foolish over. She'd worked hard to pay back each and every cent of that loan.

"That's quite the feat in the food world," Riley said as he looked over the contract, the paper version this time. Saffron had told Riley there wouldn't be a difference, and she knew he believed her, but she also knew he was thorough.

"And Saffron basically did it all on her own," Hazel interjected after being quiet for an excessive amount of time, at least for Hazel. "She's the only one of the partners who went in to work every day. And not only that, she was head chef. She created almost all of their recipes, and she always guided the sous chefs," Hazel bragged, and Saffron shot Riley an embarrassed smile.

Riley grinned back at the two women as he put the paperwork on his desk.

"The good news and the bad news are about the same. Because this contract is so poorly written, it can be deciphered in many different ways. Do you by any chance know what your partners want from you?" Riley asked as he crossed his arms over his broad chest, causing Hazel's eyes to bug out.

Saffron tried not to let her attention be derailed by Hazel's stare, but it was just too much fun to watch her friend. Hazel never ogled men. Usually, the men were falling all over themselves to catch her attention.

But Saffron needed to once again bring her focus back to Riley and his questions.

"They don't want me to leave." That was one of the few things her partners had made perfectly clear to her.

"They want to keep the status quo," Riley said more to himself than to Saffron and then added, "that means they'll probably argue that because you are the one breaking the contract, you shouldn't receive anything."

Saffron gasped as Hazel asked, "Can they do that?"

Saffron had never thought Garrett and Sanders would try to keep everything from her. She'd thought...well, she didn't know what she'd thought. But this was low, even for them.

"They can argue that. But I'll do my best to see that they won't get it. Not with the case I'll build," Riley said, and Hazel breathed a sigh of relief, but Saffron was still concerned.

"So they could take everything?" she asked.

Riley leaned forward, meeting Saffron's eyes with his own. "Nothing, when it comes to law, is a sure thing. It will depend on my case, on the judge—there are many factors, but I can promise you this. I will do everything in my power to see that doesn't happen," Riley promised.

Saffron nodded. With his assurance, she didn't feel quite as distraught as she had a few moments before. She knew things could still go south, but she had a feeling that, with Riley on her side, that wouldn't happen.

Riley looked into Saffron's eyes one more time and seemed satisfied by what he saw because he relaxed back into his seat, placing an ankle on his opposite knee.

"And now's the fun part," Riley said with a grin. "What do *you* want?"

Hazel rubbed her hands together, looking a little too gleeful, and Saffron shrugged. What *did* she want?

"I guess I want a third of what the restaurant is worth right now. It only seems fair," Saffron said as Hazel shook her head.

"You did all the work, Saff. You deserve so much more than a third. Think about it. Are you okay with Garrett and Sanders walking away with the exact same money you'll get?" Hazel asked, and Saffron pursed her lips.

"But I put them in this position. They wouldn't even be thinking about leaving," Saffron replied.

"Because they have the cushiest arrangement in the world. They let you do all the work and then see the money roll in," Hazel replied, and Saffron had to admit that was true.

"And are we really going to forget what Garrett said?" Hazel pushed, but she was right.

Garrett's words and the emotions they'd brought up in Saffron came rushing back. They hadn't wanted her. She'd been their token female. And not just that, but their token person of color. They valued her beneath themselves. Well, they wouldn't after all of this. Not if she could help it.

"I want half," Saffron said as Hazel cheered.

"Then we'll get you half," Riley's voice was able to be heard even through Hazel's uproar. "But you'll need to be ready for war."

Saffron nodded firmly. She could do this. She was strong. She deserved this. And she had great friends by her side.

She was prepared to battle.

CHAPTER EIGHT

KENZIE CLOSED the browser before Bryan caught her, yet again, researching ALS. It had been a conversation they'd had all too often the last few weeks. But Kenzie was concerned, and she wanted to be prepared. Bryan had insisted that they'd cross that bridge if and when they got there. He hadn't been diagnosed with anything as of yet, but Kenzie didn't want to cross that bridge without a plan. She was going with Bryan to his first appointment with his new doctor in Rosebud in just a few minutes, or at least she was going to drive him to the appointment, since he didn't want her to go into the actual office with him. But she wanted Bryan to go into it knowing all he could. She planned on discussing all she'd learned with him on the way to the appointment, because she wanted him to ask all the right questions and receive the right answers. Even if he would be annoyed that she'd kept researching after he'd asked her not to. But a little annoyance from Bryan would be worth it if they could finally get some real answers.

Although, Kenzie had to admit that the more she researched, the more freaked out she became. She'd known next to nothing about ALS, she'd only watched through social media as a friend of a friend battled with it, but as she'd looked things up, she'd learned quickly. The first thing that had hit her, the reason Bryan had banned her from continuing her research, was the average time of survival after diagnosis. Three to five years. Did she only have three to five years left with her husband?

Kenzie swallowed back that thought. That was definitely a bridge she wasn't ready to cross yet. But she needed Bryan to ask the doctor...

"You've been researching again, haven't you?" Bryan asked as he came into the kitchen. She'd hoped she'd look less suspicious sitting at the kitchen island with her computer instead of on the couch in their living room. There was no logic behind that idea, just hope. Evidently that hope had been misplaced.

"What?" Kenzie began to say and then met the eyes of her husband of nearly ten years. For better or worse, the man knew her inside and out...including when she was about to lie.

"Okay, but it was just quick because I wanted you to be able to ask your new doctor the right questions. And did you know that..."

"Kenzie, we talked about this," Bryan interrupted as he continued to muss his still wet hair from his shower. Kenzie loved his hair. It was one of his most attractive features. At least to her. It was the kind of hair that begged to have fingers run through it, time and time again. And Kenzie had. Did she now only have three to five years left in which to do that? She fought back the lumps that formed in her throat and stomach at the thought. The only thing keeping her from breaking down into tears was that there had been no definitive diagnosis as of yet.

"You need to ask the right questions, Bry. This is a brand-new doctor here in Rosebud. You have a chance at a fresh start. Let's go in armed with every piece of information we can, you know?" Kenzie said, trying to smile but knowing the look on her face probably made her look like a desperate raccoon. Her eyes were itchy from some of the trees in her new yard, and allergies and mascara were not the best combination. Add those to her frazzled emotions, and Kenzie knew she wasn't looking her best. But she also knew Bryan wouldn't care. He understood. He understood her.

"First, you're right. This is a brand-new doctor. A neurologist with years of experience in treating ALS. We got lucky. She's incredible. So I'm not going into this appointment armed with information to use against her."

"That wasn't what I meant."

Bryan nodded. "I know, Kenz. But I also know you and how this will go if you have your way. You're a bulldog. I love you for it. It works really well in finance and has worked for us in our marriage. But this is different. You have to let me do this my way," Bryan said as he reached out to take her hands.

Kenzie nodded even as she bit back all she wanted to say. Bryan's way had so far yielded them nothing. The doctor in San Francisco was still performing tests. Too slowly in her book. So she'd demanded Bryan get a second opinion, and when they'd found Dr. Lurker right here in Rosebud, it had felt like fate. Kenzie was thrilled.

And she got why Bryan was keeping her away. Kenzie could get overzealous. So much so that she might inhibit the doctor from being able to do her job. But she was scared. And Kenzie didn't do scared well. She'd worked hard so her life was regimented, controlled. Not up to fate in the least.

This? This illness would change everything.

"They'll start over with all the tests?" Kenzie had asked for Bryan to do that. It would cost them more, but to her, it was worth it for peace of mind. She really didn't trust the doctor Bryan had been seeing in the city. It didn't seem right to scare Bryan with ALS when it could have still been any number of things. Sure, in his professional opinion, that was most likely the case. But why already tell them? Maybe to get them ready...okay, fine. The doctor wasn't a terrible man. Even so, Kenzie wanted better. And she really felt Dr. Lurker would be better.

But she wouldn't be in the room to find out. That would just be Bryan. And she hated that he was keeping her away even as she understood why he was doing it.

"Yes, Kenz. We're starting from scratch today," Bryan promised, and she nodded. That was the best she would get.

"Then I guess we should get going?" Kenzie asked, and it was Bryan's turn to nod.

They headed out to the garage of their new home, got into Kenzie's luxury sedan, and she backed out of the garage. Their home in Rosebud was nothing like the condo they'd left behind in the city. The condo they hadn't sold yet. Kenzie wasn't sure why she was so hesitant to sell, but maybe she wanted a safe place to fall after all of this. And that condo felt safe. It was all that remained of the existence she'd worked her entire life to have. Not that she regretted moving back to Rosebud. It had been her idea. She knew it was best for her and Bry. For their marriage, for his health. But selling the condo meant...well, it meant a whole lot of things Kenzie wasn't ready to admit.

So instead of trying to replicate city living in the small town of Rosebud, she and Bryan had decided to rent an already furnished, cute little three-bedroom, ranch-style home just a few blocks from the lodge. If that was where she was going to work, might as well live close. Especially if Bryan had ALS. During her research, Kenzie had seen the type of care people with ALS required. If Bryan progressed quickly but lived a long time... Kenzie swallowed back her fear. She'd never done well with those who were ill. She hated hospitals, nursing homes, anywhere that had that smell of antiseptic and fear. She hated it all. But if she had to care for Bryan, bathe him, feed him...she drew in a deep breath. Could she do it?

"You're freaking out again," Bryan said as he put a hand over Kenzie's where it rested on the gear shift.

"I'm not...it's not..." Kenzie wanted to be brave. Bryan had kept this from her the first time around because he was worried she couldn't handle it on top of her workload. But a part of her wondered if it was more than that. Had Bryan kept it a secret because he didn't think she could handle it at *all*? And it felt like she was now proving him right with her freakouts. So then she'd try to lie and that would get them nowhere.

"I'm fine," Kenzie said after a deep breath. And, for now, she was. This appointment would go well. There wasn't much they'd be able to find out today. Today was a day for Bryan's questions, the doctor's questions, and a whole bunch of tests. The future would bring them the truth, and then they'd deal with it.

"I just wish there was a test for ALS," Kenzie muttered. That was one thing that was truly driving her batty about this entire process. There was no test for ALS. The only way to diagnose the illness was to rule everything else out. She could only imagine the amount of tests that would take, and as Bryan had pointed out, they would be a lot closer to a diagnosis had they stayed with his doctor in the city, but even that wasn't worth not getting a second opinion. Kenzie needed this second opinion.

She pulled into the parking garage attached to the hospital where Dr. Lurker's office was.

"Your chariot has arrived," Kenzie tried to joke. She wasn't the best at jokes.

"I think that's what you say when you pick me up," Bryan replied as he put an arm around Kenzie, the touch lending her so much comfort. She knew it shouldn't be this way, she should be the one offering comfort to her husband, but their marriage had always been like this. These were their roles. And ALS wanted to mess that all up. Bryan had always been so good at caring for Kenzie, so she wanted to be able to do the same for him. But what if she couldn't? What if she failed the man she loved?

"Okay. Well, remember that for then," Kenzie said, and Bryan chuckled.

"I'll be back soon," he said as he pressed a kiss to her forehead and then opened the door.

"Are you sure you don't me to go with you?" Kenzie asked, and Bryan just laughed in response as he got out of the car.

She hadn't meant it as a joke. Granted, that was often when Kenzie got her best laughs. When she wasn't meaning to be funny.

Kenzie watched as Bryan's long legs made quick work of the distance to the door that led to the elevator in the parking garage. He'd have to go to the ground floor and then walk across the driveway and into the main hospital doors. Rosebud Hospital had undergone many renovations through the years of Kenzie's life, and even the parking garage had been upgraded, but the way to get into the hospital hadn't changed.

With Bryan out of view, Kenzie's thoughts ran wild.

What would the doctor say? Did she know more than Bryan's first doctor? What if she gave the same prognosis? What if she didn't? What if Bryan had ALS?

That last question stopped her cold as shivers ran up and down her body. She turned up the heat in the car although it was spring and she lived in Northern California. But a common misconception about California was that all of it had weather like the south. And it didn't. Honestly, if one were going to compare Northern California to any of its neighbors, it was most like Oregon or maybe even Washington. But really, it had a climate all its own. The climate in the summer was usually pretty mellow; the humidity could sometimes kill you, though. But the winters often got cold—hardly ever snowy weather cold —but chilly. Sweater weather.

Kenzie was grateful thoughts of the weather had kept her occupied for a good five minutes but now she was back to thinking about Bryan. Was he to the office yet? Would they make him wait when he got there? Probably. Kenzie had never been to a doctor's appointment where she hadn't had to wait to see the doctor. So was Bryan already waiting in the examination room? Or was he still in the waiting area?

Kenzie was going to drive herself crazy. She closed her eyes, willing herself to nap. That would be the fastest way to get through this wait. But sleep wouldn't come. In fact, her thoughts just threatened to rage all the more wildly.

So she did what any sane woman living in this day and age would do. She got out her phone. She began with her emails, but now that she'd quit her job those were few and far between. What Kenzie wouldn't give to have to put out a financial fire right about now. It was her specialty. She worked great under pressure.

But alas, no fires to put out. Nothing to even scan over, because her work was kind of on hold. At least until Callie got the sellers to take their offer on the lodge. Kenzie had gotten the impression that things weren't going all that well on that front, but she trusted Callie to see things through. She always had. And she knew her friends were trying to shield her from anything that was going wrong in their not-quite-started business, considering the mess in her personal life. But now Kenzie was wishing her friends hadn't been so considerate. Maybe *she* could get the sellers to take the offer if Callie was having a tough time of it.

She was about to call Callie, her thumb hovering over

Callie's number, when she went back to her home screen. She wanted a distraction, but asking for a huge problem to be dropped in her lap wasn't fair to Bryan. Because Kenzie wouldn't be able to solve the entire problem just in the time Bryan was in this appointment, and it would carry over into time that Kenzie should be spending being a support to her husband. She needed to think about what he needed and not what she wanted. He needed a wife who would be ready for all of her concentration to be on him as soon as he got out of this appointment. Kenzie needed to be ready to take in all the doctor had said. Let it sink in. And then do some of her own research once again.

So Kenzie settled on playing a game, something she only had on her phone to pass the time while she'd waited for meetings to start at her old job. She liked the way her mind was stimulated by the word game that often took all of her mental strength to figure out.

Suddenly there was a knock on the passenger's side window, causing Kenzie to jump and her phone to fly out of her hand.

"Didn't mean to startle you," Bryan said through the glass, and Kenzie looked at the time. Had she already been waiting nearly two hours?

She quickly moved to press the unlock button for the doors before reaching toward the gas pedal where her phone had fallen.

"How did it go?" Kenzie asked while she was still bent over. She hoped he had some answers. But he might not. And she needed to be patient, be prepared for that. It wouldn't do to pepper Bryan with questions he'd only get frustrated with because he wasn't able to answer them.

"It went fine. Like I promised." Bryan grinned.

He was smiling. That was good news. Then again, Bryan

was nearly always smiling. Even before he'd gone into this appointment, he'd been smiling.

Kenzie shifted in her seat. Should she start driving? Sit there and talk with Bryan while everything was fresh in his mind? She didn't do well at not asking questions.

"She doesn't think it's ALS," Bryan said, and Kenzie felt her eyes immediately well with tears.

"What?" She needed clarification. It was just like Bryan to blurt that out without anything leading up to it.

"She's doing a number of tests, but she has a feeling one in particular will yield positive results," Bryan said. "The test for Lyme disease."

Kenzie felt her eyes pop wide open. Well, there was quite a different outlook. Lyme vs. ALS? Kenzie would take Lyme time and time again.

"She isn't sure, but she asked me about any outdoor time. The way my other doctor did. But he'd specified camping and hiking," Bryan said, and Kenzie nearly laughed. Anyone who knew Bryan knew how he felt about the outdoors. He despised it. Kenzie used to tease him about it, but now it was just life. They went to five-star restaurants and hotels. They weren't the kind of couple to trek through the woods, much less sleep in them.

"Right, Lyme comes from ticks, doesn't it?" Kenzie asked, now feeling confused. She'd felt overwhelming relief at first, but this was strange. Of all people to get Lyme disease, she would assume Bryan would be at the bottom of that list.

"Do you remember that outdoor concert we went to?" Bryan asked.

Of course Kenzie did. It had been just two months before. Right about the time Bryan had started to see...oh.

"The concert?" Kenzie asked, her voice showing the confusion she felt. It wasn't like they'd gone to some festival. It was a

Valentine's Day concert in the park. In the middle of San Francisco.

"Not exactly where you'd expect to see ticks," Kenzie said, and Bryan nodded.

"That's the reason I didn't even think to bring it up with my last doctor. But Dr. Lurker asked if I'd been in contact with any animals," Bryan said.

Kenzie sighed. The dog. The mangy stray that she'd insisted Bryan stay away from, but his big ol' heart couldn't leave it alone. He'd fed the dog and even hugged it.

"Dogs can get ticks." Kenzie remembered that much from her childhood in Rosebud. One of her neighbors had a golden retriever who loved to run away. One time he'd run into a mass of trees that grew on the outskirts of town and had come back covered in ticks.

Bryan nodded.

"So she thinks it's Lyme?"

Bryan shrugged. "The symptoms, although not traditional, do fall more in line with Lyme than with ALS. She could see why my last doctor was leaning in that direction, but after hearing about the dog, she's going to rush the Lyme test. It typically takes three to four weeks but early detection is key with Lyme."

Kenzie had already started researching on her phone and saw that what Bryan was saying was exactly what Dr. Google was telling her as well. Lyme disease, if left untreated for too long, could have lasting neurological effects.

"Can you get the antibiotics now?" Kenzie asked, hating that they'd wasted so much time. Between the move and getting an appointment with Dr. Lurker, it had been weeks since Bryan's last appointment and that had been nearly a month since the onset of Bryan's symptoms. If only that first doctor had tested for Lyme immediately and...

Kenzie shook out her arms to keep from getting any more agitated.

"Dr. Lurker doesn't think that's safe. At least not until she gets the test back. She doubts much will change between now and then, considering the disease hasn't been progressing quickly as of yet."

"But it could progress faster. Tomorrow you could wake up and bam, it would all hit?"

"What would all hit?" Bryan asked looking over Kenzie's shoulder.

"After all of this, it wouldn't even have to be ALS for you to need round-the-clock care?" Kenzie muttered. She was beyond frustrated with the medical world, and she wanted answers now. Sure Lyme was better than ALS, or so she'd assumed. But what if it was too late? What if Bryan wasn't one of these early diagnoses that Dr. Google said were so important?

"This is happy news, Kenz," Bryan said softly, but Kenzie hardly heard him. *Rush.* They were going to put a rush on his test. What did that mean? Would they hear from the doctor tomorrow? In a week? In two? If it was two, that wasn't a rush. Granted, Dr. Google and Dr. Lurker said the tests often took three to four weeks to get back.

Ugh!

"When are we supposed to hear news?" Kenzie said, and Bryan shrugged, seeming too calm.

"How can you just sit there and be so peaceful about all of this? This is why I should have gone with you. You can't just go with the flow when it comes to your life, Bry. This could change everything!"

"I'm sorry, but getting the news that I probably won't be dead in three to five years thrilled me so much that I didn't think to get the specifics on the test. Dr. Lurker, the doctor who's been seeing cases like mine for thirty years, seemed like a woman I could leave that to," Bryan said with uncharacteristic sarcasm.

"You aren't sorry at all," Kenzie huffed as she crossed her arms over her chest.

"You're right! I'm not! We went from life threatening to not. That's what I care about. But it seems like you weren't as concerned about that. Seems to me, Kenz, that your biggest fear in all of this is how it is going to alter your life. Were you thinking that at least with ALS the longest *you'll* have to suffer is three to five years? Lyme disease could leave neurological effects that I live with for decades. *Live* with, Kenz. That's all *I* needed to know," Bryan said, his voice growing louder than Kenzie had ever heard it.

"That wasn't my biggest fear," she began, but Bryan interrupted.

"Of course it was! Because like everything in our marriage, this has become all about you. *You* told me I had to go to a new doctor. *You* kept researching even though I asked you not to. I kissed you to comfort *you*. When has this not been about you? Is that what you're scared of? Our marriage will no longer revolve around you and your wants? My needs might have to become a priority?"

Kenzie couldn't believe what he was saying. Sure she'd done those things. But for *him*. Well, not the kiss of comfort part, but the rest. She'd been nothing but supportive. Kept her biggest fears to herself.

"If you hadn't gone to a new doctor, who knows how long it would have taken to get to the idea of Lyme's disease. And by that point, you might have been so far down the rabbit hole of the illness, who knows what else could be wrong?"

"Right, you saved me. Or did you save you? Because from my recollection, I'm not the one afraid of what Lyme will do to me. Sure, it won't be great, but I'd learn to live with it. It seems to me the fears we're combating right now are yours, not mine," Bryan scoffed.

Kenzie wasn't even sure she understood the words coming from his mouth. Was her sweet husband really accusing her of not caring? Or of not being willing to care for him if he was ill?

She opened her mouth to speak, but Bryan's hand shot up. "Tell me this. What scares you more? An illness that can kill me or a sickness that can maim me?"

How was that a fair question? Of course both scared her. Killing was definitely worse than maiming, but what would happen to Bryan's quality of life if he suffered from Lyme and something changed in his brain? His *brain*! It was a huge deal. Was she supposed to not be upset about that possibility?

"Wrong answer," Bryan said, and Kenzie sputtered.

"I didn't say anything!"

"You stayed silent. For nearly a minute. When the answer to that question should have been easy," Bryan said. "What happened to 'in sickness and health'?"

Kenzie shook her head. The answer had been easy, but unraveling all she was feeling took longer. Bryan was shooting questions like cannons and then seeming surprised when Kenzie wanted to clean up some of the mess those cannons were making before she fired back shots of her own.

"I just hate this situation," Kenzie finally said.

"Because my health is affecting you?" Bryan demanded.

"No!" she shouted back, hating that she was losing her cool, but he was acting so irrational. How dare he keep putting these words into her mouth!

"Bryan, this could have been solved. With one test. Had your doctor in the city asked the right questions. We wouldn't have even had the fear of ALS. You'd already have treated Lyme disease, and this would be done. This isn't about one situation being worse than another, this is that we are in this situation at all," Kenzie said, finally feeling like she was saying what she truly felt.

Bryan nodded and then met Kenzie's eyes. "But we *are* here. And I feel like I'm here alone. You want to go back in time, and that's not allowed, by physics. It feels like we should be celebrating, but you're insisting on being upset. When the worst that could happen now is so much better than the worst that could have happened before."

"If it *is* Lyme. They don't even know for sure. Not until after this test that they're supposedly rushing, but it could still be ALS."

"She doubts it."

"The other doctor doubted Lyme."

"The other doctor didn't think it *could* be Lyme."

"Because you hugged the stupid dog!" she shouted, and then the car went silent. Kenzie listened to the sounds of other cars moving around the parking garage, trying to figure out what to say into the sudden chilling quiet.

"Is that what this is about? You're blaming this on me?" Bryan finally spoke.

He wasn't wrong. This could have all been avoided.

"You didn't tell me before. I could have gone with you to that last doctor. Maybe I would have remembered the concert? And you still didn't let me go today. You're pushing me away when this affects me as much as it affects you!"

"No, it doesn't! This is my life. You can choose to walk away!"

Kenzie shook her head. In what world would she abandon her husband? Especially in his time of need?

"This is getting ridiculous," she said, starting the car.

"Would you walk away?"

"Because of all of this? Of course not!"

"Because for some reason you seemed happier when the prognosis of my illness was three to five years of life."

Were they back to this?

"You know that's not true," Kenzie said.

"So then why are you so upset now?"

"Because this could have been avoided."

"But it wasn't!"

"I know! That doesn't make me any less mad!"

"But you should be, Kenzie. You should feel so much joy at the thought of me living that you can't be mad about the rest."

"You can't tell me how to feel!"

"And you can't tell me how to interpret how you feel!"

They both fell against their respective seats, breathing hard.

"I can't help but feel you're more worried about losing a part of me than losing all of me. As if my life won't be worth living unless I'm whole."

Bryan couldn't be more wrong. Losing him would have by far been the worst thing to ever happen to her.

"I would take a part of you over none of you any day. And you should know that," Kenzie said.

"Yeah, but will you be happy with just that part?" Bryan asked, and Kenzie didn't know what to say.

"That's what I thought," Bryan said, as he opened his car door.

"Where are you going?" Kenzie asked.

"I can't stay here. I can't stay with a woman who will only stand beside me during the good times. Our life has been really great, Kenz. This is the first sign of trouble. And you're drawing away. You're protecting yourself. I need more," Bryan said, and those last words cut Kenzie. Those weren't words *her* Bryan would ever say to her. He needed more than her? It was almost as if the man speaking to her was a stranger.

It was because of those words that she let him shut the door behind him and walk back to those elevators. For a moment, she worried about him being okay on his own, but Bryan's stutters and shakes hadn't caused him to need her care as of yet. And if the doctor wasn't concerned about his progression in his illness, Kenzie knew she shouldn't be either.

The truth was, he'd be fine leaving her. She was the one who would be broken.

CHAPTER NINE

"LAUREL!" a male voice shouted from the other side of the road. Laurel had just gotten a few steps out of her car before she was accosted.

But what had she expected? News was out. Her husband had poorly invested nearly half the town's money. Although, the cops and the district attorney were saying it was much worse than that. That Bennie had taken the money of his clients and used it for himself before poorly investing the rest in hopes of recovering what he had used. And now everything was coming to light. There was no money left for anyone.

Laurel wasn't sure what to think. Especially because she hadn't really spoken to her husband in weeks. She wasn't sure why other than she knew that she was afraid. A coward. And she hated herself for it. Yet, she wasn't doing anything to change it. This state of limbo she was currently occupying seemed safer than what she was beginning to think had to be the truth. Bennie had been insisting for weeks that everything was going to be okay. The money was gone, but he'd get it back. He'd figure it out. But then the cops had shown up and arrested

Bennie, and Laurel had begun to see the holes in her husband's story. The inaccuracies she'd purposely been blind to.

Bennie was now out on bail, living in a separate room of their enormous home. So enormous, in fact, that Laurel hadn't seen her husband since he'd left jail. He'd only spent about half an hour behind bars before his lawyers got him out on bail.

He was still insisting he was innocent, but the more accusations that came, the more they made sense to Laurel. She wanted to stand by his side, but there was no denying the money was gone. And yet they still had their huge home, her designer purse collection, and way too many cars. How were they still living in the lap of luxury and yet Bennie had no way to pay back his investors? He should at least be selling their stuff. But he had insisted it wasn't so easy and they had to hold onto their assets. This message had been conveyed to Laurel through Bennie's lawyers. Because as much as she was avoiding Bennie, he was doing the same. Their house was large, but not so large that he couldn't find Laurel if he wanted to. But he hadn't. So he must not want to. And that hurt. Maybe that was another reason why she was avoiding the man she'd been married to for over half of her life.

But even though Bennie was staying away, Laurel was still living within the eye of the storm, never knowing who or what she'd collide with next. Today it looked like it would be Mr. Lind. The man from across the street who was waving her down. The man who had invested thousands, if not more, with her husband.

"Laurel," he said again and she waited for him to approach. It wouldn't be right to just ignore him.

"Hi, Mr. Lind," Laurel said weakly as she waited for him to speak. She knew going out into town would be like this. She'd driven around the outskirts of town for over an hour and yet she still didn't feel ready. She felt tired before she'd even gotten out of her car. But she'd needed groceries; eating out was a luxury she would no longer partake in, along with grocery delivery. Bennie might insist on keeping their lives the same, but Laurel just couldn't do it. So where she had control, like over her own food, she would be frugal.

"Why isn't Bennie returning my calls?" Mr. Lind asked urgently, and although Laurel hadn't spoken to her husband more than she'd had to since all of this had been revealed, she knew why Bennie wasn't calling back. Even Mr. Lind had to know why. Laurel felt it was her penance to try to give some peace to the man who had lost so much. But what could she say? The truth was Bennie wasn't going to call him back. His money was gone.

"I'm so sorry," was all Laurel could think to say.

"Why are you sorry? What did you do?" Mr. Lind began to get aggravated, and she realized she'd said the wrong thing. Was there even a right thing to say right now?

"Hey, Mr. Lind," Hazel's clear voice sounded behind Laurel before she nestled her way into the middle of the conversation. "How's your beautiful wife doing?"

Mr. Lind seemed thrown off by the question and paused.

"Laurel here has some things to get done, but we'll see you again soon. Have a great day!" Hazel pulled Laurel behind her, away from the grocery store.

"I need groceries," Laurel explained, trying to get her arm back but Hazel shook her head.

"You need to get home. Now." Hazel opened the door to her car and pushed Laurel in before going around to the driver's seat.

"What? Why?" Laurel asked, feeling like she was living in a fog that hadn't lifted ever since she'd heard the news that Bennie had lost the money of so many of her friends and some of her family.

"The cops are there. They're freezing your assets and seizing your home. At least, according to what I heard," Hazel said.

As Laurel tried to wrap her mind around the actual words, her brain wandered. It was almost as if it couldn't handle the actual news so it was latching on to parts of the conversation that didn't count. Like how did Hazel know what was going on before Laurel did? Bennie hadn't even bothered to call. Even though she knew he was home. Hazel had always been great at knowing the gossip before it even started in the rumor mill. And now Laurel was that gossip. Huh. Who would have thought?

"Laurel. Laurel!" Hazel shouted, and her loud voice penetrated the fog.

"You need to get in there and get your personal items. Think of it like a fire. What can you not live without?" Hazel asked, and Laurel shrugged.

Her kids had taken most of their mementos when they'd moved out. Laurel thought about her husband, but it looked like he was only looking out for himself during this fire. Sure, the man had never been the most attentive of mates, but to leave Laurel out in the cold at a time like this? When this mess was his making? Laurel wasn't sure what to make of that. Her foggy head didn't allow much thought.

"Your grandma's quilt." Hazel pulled Laurel from her thoughts again.

Right. That was priceless.

"I'll need my file on the charity event I'm putting on next month," Laurel said, and Hazel shook her head.

"Babe, I don't think you'll need to be worrying about that," Hazel said.

Laurel looked at her friend, her eyes wide. What could she mean?

"They got Sadie Logan to take over for you," Hazel replied softly.

Laurel felt tears prick her eyes. Really, this is what she was going to cry over? She'd hardly cried since the mess had all started, and yet she was going to cry that the country club had found someone else to take over her spot as chairwoman for a charity event? Laurel was losing her mind.

"I'm sure Sadie will need your help," Hazel offered, but Laurel wasn't so sure. The Logans had lost money in Bennie's investments as well.

"They all hate me," Laurel said quietly, and Hazel shook her head.

"No breaking down right now, girl. You've got to get in that house and get what you need and get out," Hazel said with the firmness of a military general.

Get in and get out. But why was she going in? And where could she go once she got out? She asked Hazel that question.

"We've got that all taken care of. So you just focus your pretty little head on what you need to do, okay?" Hazel said as she turned onto Laurel's street and her house came into view. But Laurel's eyes weren't on her house. They were on the dozen cop cars with flashing lights surrounding her house. Men and women were walking out of her home, carrying paintings, her shoes, her purses.

"Don't worry about clothes," Hazel said as she parked as close as she could get to Laurel's house without crashing into a cop car. "What do you need?"

"The quilt," Laurel said. "The portrait the kids painted me for Mother's Day. The jewelry tray Rex made me when he was in second grade."

"Got it. Anything made by your kids or your grandma," Hazel said, her tone and gaze all business.

Laurel nodded as Hazel turned to her, taking her face in her hands.

"I need you to focus, Laurel. This is going to be rough. But you will lose everything if you don't focus right here. Those things you're talking about. They have no value other than sentimental. You have every right to take them. We won't let the cops stop us, got it?"

"But we're criminals. We don't have rights," Laurel muttered, and Hazel groaned.

"Bennie is the criminal. And even he has rights. Now focus," she said sternly, and Laurel nodded. Focus. She wasn't a criminal. She had rights.

She threw the car door open and stomped up the grass to her front door, which was standing wide open, Hazel behind her every step of the way.

"Get your stuff," Hazel commanded, and Laurel walked forward, bypassing cops who were all eyeing her suspiciously. But no one said anything.

So far, so good.

"You can't be here," a voice even sterner than Hazel's said, and Laurel froze.

"This is her home," Hazel responded because Laurel still couldn't speak.

"Not for long," another voice said as others snickered, but the first voice cleared his throat and all laughter silenced.

Hazel physically turned Laurel so she was facing the man who had spoken. Unlike most of the other people in the room, this man wasn't wearing a uniform. He wore a blue button-up and slacks. He looked professional, and he looked like the man in charge.

"Just let her get her stuff, please," Hazel said as she pulled Laurel into a side hug.

"I can't..." the man began.

"I'm not sure what you guys are doing, but you can't have a use for stuff like her grandma's quilt or the gifts her kids made for her, right?" Hazel said, and the man narrowed his eyes as he took in first her and then Laurel.

Laurel swallowed. She was losing everything. She could feel it. Her entire life was crashing down around her, and she wondered what she'd done to deserve this. She'd been blind to her husband's work. That was for sure. And she'd been all too happy to spend his money without asking where it was coming from. She never saw the finances and was pleased with the easy way her marriage had worked.

"Hammond," the stern man said, and a man in uniform appeared.

"Take Mrs. Stockton and her friend to...her bedroom?"

Laurel nodded. Everything that mattered to her would be there.

"She's taking a few personal items. Look them over to be sure they aren't pertinent to the case, and if they aren't let them go," the man in the blue button-up commanded, and Hammond nodded before waving to the stairs.

Laurel scurried up the steps and then down the familiar hall to her bedroom. Would this be the last time she would walk these same steps? This had been her home for nearly twenty years. Their dream home. The one she and Bennie had designed from the ground up.

But she pushed those thoughts away. Right now, what mattered were those items. The ones Hazel had fought so hard for her to be able to keep.

Laurel ran into the bathroom to get the jewelry dish and then spotted a few other ceramic items that her kids had made in her room. She took down a few family photos and then went to the linen closet to get the quilt. Lastly, she found the portrait her kids had all had a part in creating and then passed the items to Hammond. He looked over each thing and handed them all back.

"Good luck, Mrs. Stockton," Hammond said quietly as Laurel left the room.

She smiled gratefully at the cop. She would take any luck offered at this point.

Only when she had set her priceless parcels in the backseat and taken her spot next to Hazel did she remember the next part of her plan. Well, more precisely, that she had no plan. Laurel covered her face with her hands, but she needed to be braver than she wanted to be. She needed to look to her future even though she felt like she didn't have one. Thankfully, Hazel was right here by her side, ready to take care of all the details. How had Laurel gotten so lucky?

"Where to now?" Laurel asked through her hands as Hazel flipped a U-turn and drove back along Laurel's street to the main road.

"Callie's," Hazel said as she turned at the end of the street. "I wanted to keep you with me, but Callie said you wouldn't be up for staying in a place with rambunctious teenagers. I told her the use of *rambunctious* was spot on."

Laurel smiled. She was smiling. That was good. Now that she'd come out of her house with what really mattered, some of the fog didn't feel so heavy. And yet there were still other parts that seemed impenetrable.

"She also pointed out that you two wear the same size clothing and shoes, so it will all be one big slumber party," Hazel said, and Laurel shook her head.

"It's bad enough to have to impose on her hospitality, but I won't take Callie's clothes," she said firmly, but Hazel just laughed.

"Have you seen Callie's closets? No one woman needs all that clothing. Even the two of you won't make a dent in that collection," Hazel replied.

"But..."

"But nothing. You can't continue to wear that same outfit day in and day out, and who knows when your stuff will be released."

If it would be released. Laurel had avoided trying to understand what could happen next because of her fear, but the lawyers had mentioned something about their assets possibly being seized. They had never said anything about them being *un*seized. Burying her head in the sand hadn't been the best tactic, but Laurel had had no idea how to face life these days. Especially with this fog that just wouldn't go away.

"What if..."

"We'll deal with what ifs later," Hazel said as she pulled into Callie's driveway.

The door to Callie's home opened immediately, and Callie ran barefoot down her walkway and to Hazel's car. She threw Laurel's door open and pulled her into the safest hug Laurel had felt in a long time. Soon she felt another pair of arms and knew Hazel had joined as well.

"You will be okay," Hazel promised, and in that moment in the arms of her friends, Laurel believed that maybe she really would be.

CHAPTER TEN

—————————

"SHE'S ASLEEP," Hazel whispered as she joined Callie in the kitchen. She didn't need to—Callie didn't live in a mansion but there was no way to hear even raised voices from the kitchen all the way in her guest bedroom upstairs. Especially since Callie had made up the furthest guest bedroom for Laurel.

"One fire down, a few more to go," Callie said as Hazel nodded. Hazel knew she wasn't just there to deliver Laurel, although what she'd been able to do with that situation was a godsend. Callie wasn't sure how Hazel knew just where to find Laurel when they'd gotten the news that Laurel's possessions were being seized, but she had, somehow. And she had gotten Laurel in and out of her home with the stuff that mattered without seeing her husband. Callie called that a good day's work. But they had much more to do.

"I thought at least some part of my plan would go well," Hazel said, and Callie frowned.

"I take it offering Jim and Sue a private concert didn't go well?" Callie asked, and Hazel shook her head, her eyebrows lifted in confusion.

"Who would have thought I would have made a mortal

enemy of the one person in the world who wasn't a Wells Harrington fan?" Hazel said as she took the bar stool next to Callie.

"I'm sure you have more than one enemy," Callie teased with a grin, trying to lighten the mood even though her stomach was twisted up in knots. Without the lodge...no. She couldn't think like that. They were going to get this. They had to. They just needed to figure out a new game plan.

Hazel nudged Callie in the ribs, causing the latter to laugh, and Hazel joined her.

"You're right though," Hazel said as her fingers followed the lines in the dark pattern on Callie's granite countertop.

"Hey. No long face. We all have enemies," Callie said when she realized her joke had been taken seriously. The last thing she wanted was to hurt Hazel's feelings. Hazel had worked a near miracle with Laurel, but that didn't mean Callie should expect that she could work one with Sue and Jim as well. Callie figured the work and the proverbial ball were now back in her court. And she'd figure it out. She did this for a living day in and day out. Problems far worse than this had been thrown her way before.

"Yeah, but none of *your* enemies are keeping us from achieving our dream," Hazel said as she turned to look at Callie.

"*Our* dream?" Callie said, a smile coming over her face. Although they'd all called the lodge that when they were eighteen, Callie had started to think she was the only one who still saw it like that. But with those words, she knew that Hazel was truly on board. That was a tiny miracle in and of itself.

"Of course. I know you had to strong-arm a few of us into this, but, Callie, you have to know that I'm grateful. That we're all grateful. I need this so badly in my life right now, and out of the five of us, I might need it the least."

Callie nodded because she felt in that same boat. Laurel,

Saffron, and Kenzie were battling some of life's hardest challenges, and the lodge seemed like the only reprieve for all three of them.

"What else can we do? We have to get the lodge," Hazel said firmly, and Callie looked down at her laptop, ready to get to work. But as she began to type, she realized that this work environment just wouldn't do. She needed to get to her office where she had all of her resources right at hand. Where she had her assistant a room away.

She looked back toward her stairs. Could she leave Laurel all alone on a day like today?

"I think she'd appreciate the alone time instead of finding us hovering when she wakes up," Hazel responded to Callie's thoughts. She had somehow always done that. Hazel's adversaries liked to paint her as a person who only looked out for number one. Who was too loud and brash to see anything beyond herself, but that wasn't the case at all. Those who knew and loved Hazel were able to see this part of her. The woman was in tune with those in need, and her empathy was pretty powerful. Callie had long ago stopped asking Hazel how she knew what Callie was thinking.

"You're right," Callie said as she remembered how Laurel had ducked her head the moment they'd finished hugging, almost as if she wasn't ready to face even her friends yet. Not that Callie blamed her.

"Then I think I'll go into the office for a few hours. See what I can work out," Callie said, gathering her laptop and slipping it into her gigantic purse.

"Call me when you find a solution? Or come across another problem? Or need to bounce an idea past someone?" Hazel said as she stood, and Callie laughed as she joined Hazel in her walk to the front door. Callie would lock it behind her friend before going out of her kitchen and into her garage.

"I promise to call you if anything at all arises. And thanks again for helping Laurel." Callie drew Hazel into a hug Callie knew she would hate. As empathetic as Hazel was, she was not affectionate. At least not physically. Of course, she'd give a hug in the most dire of circumstances, like when Laurel had arrived at Callie's home, but when it wasn't absolutely needed and especially when it was just for Hazel's sake? She hated it. And it made Callie adore giving them all the more.

Hazel pushed off of Callie immediately after the hug was given, but her smile was nearly as large as Callie's as she walked out the front door.

Callie glanced up the stairs one more time after locking her front door and heard nothing coming from the far guest room. Laurel had been in her home enough times to know exactly where to find anything she'd need. Callie left a quick note on the fridge, telling Laurel she'd better grab something to eat, and then Callie was off for the office.

The drive between her home and her office was a quick one and she was soon walking into the cute space that she'd designed with Hazel's help. It had been about fifteen years since Callie had decided to go off on her own. It was one of the smartest moves of her life, because being on her own gave her the courage to not only sell real estate but buy some for herself. She developed a small parcel at first and then started buying bigger and bigger. She was now one of the leading real estate agents in Northern California along with being a land developer. It was a lot of work for her little five-woman operation, but Callie's team was the best of the best.

"Hey, Sydney," Callie called out to her assistant and right-hand woman as she walked past Sydney's desk, situated just outside of Callie's office. There was one other office off the main waiting area that belonged to the three other women who worked for Callie. Their adorable little waiting room was full of greenery that Sydney worked hard to keep alive and dark-brown furniture. It had been a bit masculine for Hazel's taste, but Callie had wanted to keep it that way because most agents in her industry were male. She didn't want them to feel like they'd been swallowed up by cupcakes and roses when they walked into her office. The photos on the walls were all of the nearby Redwood State Park, but she did keep the walls a stark white to brighten up the place, and she had allowed Hazel to put white frilly curtains over the windows. Overall the space was perfect for what Callie needed.

"Do you want your messages?" Sydney asked as she followed Callie into her office with a mug of herbal tea, Callie's preferred drink in the afternoon.

Callie nodded as she took the tea from her assistant and offered her thanks.

"You're welcome," Sydney said before listing off a number of calls that Callie would need to return.

"Got it," Callie took a sip of her tea after she'd finished taking notes on the messages Sydney had relayed. "Can you email Murphy the spreadsheet on the Escalante deal?" Callie asked, and Sydney nodded.

"Thanks, Sydney," Callie said as her assistant left the office and Callie got to work. She returned the calls she needed to, emailed other callers, and hours had passed before she could finally concentrate on the reason why she'd come in. The lodge.

She really would have to consider hiring one or maybe two more people for her company if she was going to be spending more time doing lodge business. Callie's office worked like clock-work for the time being, but that was only when she did a big chunk of the work. She'd need to get some of that off her plate before she took on a huge new project. And even though the idea of handing off some of what she did to someone else scared her, she knew it would be worth it. For years, in the back of her mind, she'd always intended for the lodge to be the pinnacle of her career. And getting to reach that peak with her best friends? Incredible.

"Will you be needing anything else this evening?" Sydney asked, peeking her head into Callie's office. Callie looked up at the clock that already read seven P.M. Where had the day gone?

"I'm sorry. You should have left an hour ago," Callie said, but Sydney shook her head.

"I had a lot to do. I would have said something otherwise," Sydney said with a sassy pump of her eyebrows, and Callie didn't doubt it. The young woman had been timid when she'd first come to work for Callie but now knew how to not only voice her opinion when asked for it but also her concerns anytime they arose. And Callie appreciated that. In fact, maybe she'd hire from within. Promote Sydney and then find a new assistant?

"And I'm good. You go home to that family of yours," Callie said with a grin that Sydney returned. Sydney was mom to three adorable little girls and wife to one very adoring husband. Sydney loved their work, but her true pride and joy was her little family.

"Oh, and please tell Millie good luck tomorrow," Callie called as Sydney began to close Callie's door.

"Will do!" Sydney said just as the door closed.

Sydney's oldest had just begun gymnastics and would be taking part in her very first meet the next morning. According to Sydney, Millie was a ball of nerves, but Callie was sure the little girl would rock it. She'd seen a few of Millie's routines, the ones she could do in her backyard, and she was quite impressive. Especially for a seven-year-old.

From the window that gave her a view into the main area of their office space, Callie noticed the light went off and realized she was the last one there. Sydney only ever turned off that main light when the other three women who worked with them had already left for the day. But Callie was quite used to burning the midnight oil alone.

And now that all of her distractions were gone, it was time for her to get to work. She pulled out all of the paperwork having to do with the lodge deal, everything she could find. She was going to go over it with a fine-toothed comb. She would find something she could work with. She had to.

Before she got too far into her work, Callie ordered some takeout from a nearby Chinese restaurant that she frequented on her late nights at work. It was a little sad that every person who worked in that place knew her by name. But a woman had to eat, especially when she was working late. And Callie knew that if she really got started on her work without calling in that order, she'd never come up for air and she'd end up going the whole night without any sustenance. And while that might have worked for a younger Callie, wiser and maybe a little older Callie knew how much better she worked with some food in her belly.

The food arrived ten minutes later, and Callie was off. She read over each individual piece of correspondence and then the offer she and her friends had put in. She read the listing and all of the information she'd been able to get from the sellers and their agent. By the time she'd finished her dinner, she was about halfway through and was ready to power on. She finally finished reading everything and looked up at the clock in her office, which now read two A.M.

She sighed, trying not to feel discouraged because in all that time she had found nothing. Zilch. But she wasn't giving up. She'd start at the beginning and would go through it all again.

CALLIE SAT up as light streamed in through her office window from the outside world. She pulled off a piece of paper that was attached to her face as her eyes adjusted to the light. What time was it?

She looked up at her clock and sat up straighter. Eight A.M.?

Oh, good heavens, she'd fallen asleep. She turned her neck this way and that to try to crack it. Another lesson she'd learned since her younger years was never to fall asleep at her desk. Callie would be suffering the consequences all day. And for what? She still had nothing. The lodge seemed even further out of reach than it had been the day before.

Callie drew in a deep breath, fighting off the feelings of failure that threatened. So she didn't have a plan...yet. But she could still...

No. She had to admit defeat. Because as much as she didn't want it to be true, they'd tried everything. And if the sellers wouldn't sell, what could Callie do? She could continue to fight all she wanted, but she was battling in a circle and would always wind up just where she'd began. She had nothing left to give to this. No other angles, no other tactics. She'd exhausted all of them. She'd dug through her bag of tricks, but there was no getting around this one. Callie knew the developer would be coming in with his offer in just a couple of days. And then the lodge would be gone to them forever. Their dream would be bulldozed.

Callie shook the melancholy away as she stood, telling herself she only felt beaten because she'd slept at her desk. But there had to be some other solution. She might have been ready to admit defeat a moment before, but after a shower and maybe a nap, the world would seem brighter. She sniffed herself and then nodded. She definitely needed that shower.

Thankfully, it was a Saturday, so the office wouldn't be

filling with people at any moment. She could do her walk of shame in privacy. Well, somewhat privately, considering one of the most frequented diners in Rosebud was just across the street. That place would be positively bursting at eight on a Saturday morning.

She gathered her things and went for the door, locking up before walking toward her car. Although the morning was chilly, it was the nice kind of chilly with a crispness to it that had her anticipating the day and almost forgetting that her dream was practically in the toilet.

She was still a few steps from her car when she heard her name being called from across the street. That dang diner.

She looked up to see Matt and his wife waving, their preteen kids looking between Callie and their parents, who stood in their way of getting into the diner.

"Hey Matt, Vivi!" Callie called with a smile and then walked a few steps backward, bumping into her car.

Thank goodness. She needed to get out of there before she saw anyone else she knew. Granted, seeing Matt was maybe already the worst-case scenario. No one wanted to see their ex after a night of sleeping on their desk.

Matt pointed, and Callie could tell he was telling Vivi and the kids to go on without him before he jogged across the street.

Great. Just great.

Callie watched Vivi as she ushered the kids into the diner, smiles on all three of their faces, and for just a moment, she thought of how that could have been her. Matt had proposed to her, after all. If she had just said yes...but, no. This was her life. She'd chosen her career. Because she had known Matt didn't just want marriage, he wanted kids, a wife that wasn't also married to her job, the whole nine yards. But Callie couldn't give that to him. Not when she'd just started out on her own. That fledgling real estate company was her baby. She couldn't afford another one. So they'd parted ways, as friends. Matt had been understanding. He knew proposing had been a long shot. But he'd tried because he'd wanted her to choose him. Instead, she'd chosen her work.

Her baby that was kind of failing her at the moment, considering her situation with the lodge. Given the chance, would she make that same choice again? She had to believe she would. She loved her job, even with its bad days, but she couldn't help but wonder what if? What if she had chosen Matt?

"You aren't just leaving the office, are you?" Matt asked as he came to a stop in front of Callie.

His blond hair gleamed in the morning light, and his eyes were bright not just because of the sunshine but because they were brimming with happiness. Those characteristics were still the same fifteen years later. Matt had always been one of the cheeriest people she'd known. It was what had first attracted her to the man. Callie's life had needed some more sunshine.

But there were a few small physical changes to the man she'd once loved. What had once been a washboard stomach had given way to a dad gut, and his arms weren't quite as beefed up as they had once been. Even with all of that, Callie thought the years had been kind to Matt. He looked like the man he'd wanted to be. A content dad, a doting husband.

"Um, I forgot something last night and..." Callie didn't finish her lie. She knew Matt wasn't buying it.

"I fell asleep at my desk," she admitted, and Matt laughed.

"That explains the pen marks on your face," he said with a smirk, and Callie began wiping at her cheek. Of all the days...

"I'm just kidding," Matt said.

Callie didn't even think before she slugged him in the arm.

Matt grunted. "Still got a wicked right hook, huh?"

"And don't you forget it," Callie said crossing her arms, making Matt laugh once again.

"You need to take care of yourself, Cal," Matt said softly, and Callie knew he was coming from a good place. He'd cared for her in a way no one else had. Maybe in a way no one else would. That thought was depressing. Sure, her parents cared but they supported her ambition one hundred percent. Matt had always been the one to look out for her personal well-being, along with her friends. Laurel, especially, had been good at that too.

"I am," Callie said and then amended, "or I mostly am. Last night was a one-time thing."

"So you start work at nine and you're off at six?" Matt asked. "You take weekends off?"

"Close enough," Callie said as she cracked her neck again. She really needed that shower and a couple of ibuprofen. She could feel a massive headache coming on.

"Okay," Matt said, knowing there was only so much pushing he could do with Callie. "You know taking care of yourself isn't the same thing as taking it easy?"

Callie nodded her head. She did get that. It was just hard for her to put it into practice.

"Good," Matt said before rubbing his belly. "Well, I'm starving so..."

"Have a nice breakfast. Tell Vivi and the kids I said hi."

"I will. Take care of yourself," Matt admonished one more time before jogging back to the diner.

Callie got into her car and set her purse in the seat beside her. It was the only thing to have taken that seat in a long time. Callie didn't often drive anyone around beside the odd client here and there. The sedan wasn't exactly a family car, but it was made for five. And only one person ever used it.

She thought about her big house. Laurel was there now, but it was typically empty as well. Her big yard was never played in. Callie had only been pleased with the yard for resale value. She didn't have any siblings with kids, and her friends' kids were now too old to play in a yard. And Callie would probably never have any children of her own. She'd never felt the ticking of her biological clock, so she'd assumed she didn't have one. Some people were made to have kids, and Callie wasn't. Was she?

She suddenly yearned for more in her life. To be going home to someone besides her friend who needed a place to stay. To someone who made her house their home. She didn't long for crying babies or long nights. But maybe loud cartoons on a Saturday morning? Maybe a game of catch in her backyard? But one came with the other. She couldn't long for the playing but none of the baby stuff. Kids didn't work like that. Besides with the big 5-o just around the corner, Callie's childbearing years were in her rearview, weren't they? Technically, physically, she could do it. She hadn't been through the Change, as her mother liked to call it, but...it all felt too ridiculous to even consider.

Stop, she told herself. She needed to focus on one impossible task at a time. She needed to get that lodge.

Callie pulled into her driveway and then into her garage, pushing the clicker in her car in order to close the massive door behind her. Her life was good. She'd worked hard to be just where she was. Sure, she was bummed about the lodge. That had to be what was bringing on these waves of sentiment. She was fine. She'd go inside to her friend and enjoy their time together. She wouldn't have been as available for Laurel had Callie had her own person or people to be worried about. Callie was free as a bird. She could fly at the drop of a hat.

But what if she was sick of flying?

CHAPTER ELEVEN

HAZEL ROLLED over to look at the clock beside her bed. Eight-thirty A.M. Just as she thought. Much too early on a weekend morning for there to be noise in her home, considering the only people who lived there were herself and two teenagers. There weren't too many great things about moody teenagers, but one major point in Hazel's book was their ability to sleep in. Especially since she matched it.

But no, there it was again. Definite moving of things. Which child of hers was moving things at eight-thirty on a freaking Saturday morning?

Hazel kicked off her covers and walked down the hall, past the staircase and then stopped. In front of her were the two doors to each of her boys' bedrooms, and both were closed. She was going to assume one was sleeping and one was making the ruckus.

She turned to open Sterling's door, since he was the obvious choice. Chase hadn't seen the hours before noon on a Saturday in years, but then the noise came again. From Chase's room.

Hazel knocked once and didn't wait for an invitation before

opening the door. The boys got a warning that she was coming, but that was all that she would give them. She had told them this was her home. They were being given a room each to use in the way they wanted, but the rooms still belonged to Hazel, giving her full access to them anytime she wanted.

It was a tactic she'd seen on a parenting Instagram, a way to keep your kids from feeling too entitled, but it hadn't gone over well in her home. However, Hazel had stuck to her guns, and what were her kids going to do? Buy their own homes?

When Hazel opened the door, she wasn't sure what she'd been expecting, but what she saw made her mouth drop open. What in the heck?

Two suitcases filled the open expanse of Chase's carpet. One was already full with clothes, and he was trying to fit his skateboard along with his video game console in the other.

"What are you doing?" Hazel asked, and she realized Chase hadn't even looked up.

When he turned, she could see the white item filling his ear that had kept him from hearing her. Chase had always listened to his music way too loudly.

Hazel marched across the room, and Chase saw her just at the moment she went to yank out the air pod from his ear.

"Mom!" Chase yelped as Hazel crossed her arms over her chest. He wasn't the one who deserved to yelp. Not when he was standing here...packing? Is that what he was doing?

"Chase Leo Harrington, you had better tell me what the heck is going on here before I whoop that booty of yours," Hazel said, suddenly drawing on her years in the South. Sure, she hadn't been born and raised there, but the twenty plus years of living there had given Hazel her very own dose of southern sass.

Chase rolled his eyes.

"And if you so much as try to roll your eyes again...!"

"I'm moving, Mom," Chase said in the same way he would have told his mother he was going to the movies. Her sixteen-year-old son thought he could just announce that he was moving.

"Where?" Hazel said as she raised her hands in the air and then dropped them again.

"To Dad's. He said I could," Chase said, and Hazel scoffed.

She didn't care what Chase's father had said. She had a court document that said Chase was staying right here until he turned eighteen. And so help her, he was going to enjoy every minute of it.

"I've already called an Uber; Dad bought me a plane ticket last night," Chase explained, and Hazel realized this wasn't just some teenage rebellion. Chase, with his father, had planned this out.

Hazel rubbed her temples. It was too early, and she hadn't had the coffee she needed to deal with this situation.

"Unpack your bags. You are going nowhere," Hazel commanded as she turned to leave the room.

"You can't make me stay here!" Chase shouted, and Hazel heard Sterling's door open.

"Yes, I can. I have a very legitimate document from a judge that says I can," Hazel said, trying to keep her cool.

"I hate it here, and I hate you! You can't make me live with you. I want to live with Dad!" Chase continued shouting, and his words stung Hazel in just the way he wanted them to. She tried to remind herself that Chase didn't truly understand what he was saying, that he was just angry, but the words still hurt.

"You haven't even given Rosebud a chance," Hazel began but was cut off.

"We've lived here for over a month. It's not getting any better. It's getting worse. The school here is stupid, there isn't a decent skate park, and everything closes at nine P.M.!"

The first two were the same arguments, almost word for word, that Hazel had shouted at her own parents when she was sixteen. She'd been suffocating.

But this was different. Chase had already lived elsewhere. Being in a small town for part of his teenage years would do him some good.

"You can't make me stay, Mom. I'm a human being. I have rights," Chase said.

"When you're eighteen." Hazel muttered.

But those had been the wrong words. Fire blazed in Chase's eyes. "I...AM...LEAVING!"

Hazel was pretty sure all of their neighbors had just heard those words.

"Where, Chase? I'm going to call your dad, and he'll side with me. Being here is what is best for you and your brother," Hazel said with a shake of her head.

"No, Dad said he's on my side. He said I can live with him if you'd let me. It's all your fault I'm here. Just let me go and let me be happy. Can't you see I'm miserable here?"

"Chase, give it more time."

"I gave it time! I still hate it. And every second I'm here, I hate you more. I don't want to hate you, Mom," Chase said, and it was those words that caused a fissure in the wall Hazel had put up during this argument.

She needed a moment away. A moment to think. A moment to rail on Wells. How dare the man tell their son it was her fault all of this had happened? He was the one who'd demanded a divorce. Not the other way around.

Hazel walked out of Chase's room and nearly ran into Sterling.

"Is Chase really going to move?" he asked.

"Yes!" Chase shouted for her, so Hazel just pulled her

younger son into her arms before placing a kiss on his curly head.

"I'm going to call your dad," she said to Sterling in lieu of an answer. She wanted to say *no* with assurance, but what if...no, she wouldn't let her sixteen-year-old move across the country. But she wouldn't tell Sterling that unless she knew for sure. And right now, Chase was a bit too sure that he was moving for Hazel to be sure about anything.

Hazel marched to her room, feeling her anger swirl within her. A heads-up would have been nice. Wells had obviously talked to Chase the night before, and she hadn't gotten so much as a text from the man she'd been married to for over half of her life.

She programmed her phone to call Wells and then pressed the phone to her ear.

"Before you start, Hazel," Wells began without even a *hello*.

At least he'd learned something over the years they'd been married. He needed to get his words out while he could. And because Hazel was just a little impressed with his tactic, she decided to let him have his say. She'd have hers in a minute.

"He called me crying. When have you seen Chase cry?" Wells asked.

Hazel couldn't remember. It had been at least four years. Maybe longer.

"He's falling apart, Hazel. He misses his friends, his home. He doesn't know anyone there. He's feeling lost."

"And whose fault is that?" Hazel asked, throwing the argument that had always won for her in Wells's face right from the start. He asked for the divorce, and he'd gotten it. But he was going to feel every last consequence.

"We needed this. You know that. Even the kids know that. We're much better off apart," Wells said slowly, and Hazel hated that he was right.

"Chase is reeling from the divorce and now moving; it's too much on him," Wells said.

"We agreed the boys needed to stay together. That I'd keep them here," Hazel reminded.

"I know," Wells said in his infuriatingly slow way. The drawl, while sometimes sexy, was beyond frustrating during an argument. *Just say the words*, she always wanted to shout. Sometimes she did. "But it was more *you* said it and I had to agree."

Wells was right again. Why, during this argument that meant more to her than any other, was Wells right?

"He's a kid. *We're* supposed to decide what's best for him," Hazel said, and by the rustling on the other end, she was pretty sure Wells was shaking his head.

"I can't see you. What did your neck just say for you?" Hazel asked.

"He's sixteen. Hardly a kid. And he absolutely knows what he wants," Wells replied aloud.

"But is it what he needs?" Hazel countered. "He needs his family."

"He'd have me."

"What about his mother and his brother?"

"He'd visit you. As often as either of you want."

"It's not the same."

"You told me it should be enough for me."

"You tore our family apart!" Hazel yelled.

"I had to," Wells muttered.

The man had hardly ever stood up to Hazel in their twenty-plus years of marriage. But he had for the divorce and now this. But Hazel couldn't let Chase go. A boy should be with his mother.

"You could always move back with him," Wells said but Hazel knew she couldn't. Sterling, unlike his brother, was thriving here. Exactly what she'd hoped would happen for both of her boys. Sterling had made friends, not a ton, but a good number, and that was better than what he'd had in Nashville. He was already doing a few AP classes, and his teachers loved him. He'd just joined the chess club, so, no, a move back to Nashville wouldn't be fair to Sterling.

Chase had had all of that in Nashville, but like a whirlwind, Hazel had decided they needed to go. Chase was the kind to thrive anywhere. Except he wasn't thriving in Rosebud. Not yet. But with more time...

"Give it another month," Hazel said.

"He says he can't do another day. Hazel, I know you don't like this, but it's Chase. You know how he gets when his mind is set on something. If he doesn't come here, I'm afraid of what lengths he'll go to in order to get out of there."

Chase wouldn't run away. Except Hazel had seen the challenge in his gaze. She knew that look because she'd given it to her parents, Wells, anyone who dared to defy her. Chase was going to leave. Somehow, someway. Didn't she prefer to know where he was?

Of course. But could she really just let him go?

"He needs this, Hazel." Wells must have sensed he was wearing her down.

"You should have talked to me first," Hazel said, tears filling her eyes.

"I know. But you needed to see his determination first hand."

Hazel pursed her lips as some of her tears fell. She blinked them away and then rubbed her cheeks free of them.

"He comes home every other weekend," Hazel demanded.

"Done," Wells replied.

"I have a say in the rules in your home. Your new girlfriend isn't allowed to throw any of her parties with those scantily clad friends of hers. Your home is no longer a party house. You are no longer just a country music star. You are a dad, first and foremost. Chase and his well-being come before your career and before your girlfriend."

"I promise." Wells hadn't even hesitated. Hazel had known he wouldn't. He was a good dad. Sure, he'd blown off steam with his girl after his family had left but Hazel knew Chase would be his priority.

"Fine," Hazel whispered as tears threatened again. However, she needed to hold it together. "But for the record, I hate this."

"Noted," Wells said. "For the record, I hate that you're hurting."

And this was why, no matter what he'd done, Hazel couldn't despise Wells. They had been broken beyond repair; he'd just been the one brave enough to point it out and then take on all of Hazel's anger. Really, she admired the man, but she still kind of disliked him as well.

"I'll get him on that plane. But he'll be back here in two weeks," Hazel said.

"And I'll get him on *that* plane," Wells promised. "And, Hazel? Thank you."

Hazel bit her lip to keep from crying. Why was Wells being so nice about this? That only served to make things harder. She'd rather rail and yell. But the answer to that question was easy. Wells was being nice because he knew this was killing her and he still cared about her. So because of that, and because she knew she'd truly lost—there was no one and nothing left to fight against—Hazel was done yelling.

"I need to go," Hazel said.

"I'll take care of him," Wells promised before Hazel hung up.

She drew in a deep breath before leaving her room. She was about to make one son's dreams come true while having to explain to the other son that his brother was leaving them. And do it all while she disagreed with what was happening. But Wells was right. She had to let Chase go or he'd make her let him go. And the former would be better than the latter. Even knowing that, Hazel didn't want to do it. But she would.

Man, parenting sometimes sucked.

CHAPTER TWELVE

"AND CALLIE DIDN'T TELL us any of this?" Saffron asked as she closed her laptop. She'd invited Laurel over for dinner that evening and had been surprised when she'd accepted. Typically when things blew up, and boy, had Laurel's life blown up, Laurel was known to find the nearest bunker and hide out until everything was better. So because she was still in the midst of all of the mess, Saffron had been sure Laurel would still be hiding out. The cops were still in and out of her home, the prosecutor had her on speed dial, and there were rumors that Bennie was headed straight for prison. So inviting Laurel to dinner had been more of an "I'm here for you" gesture. Saffron hadn't thought that Laurel would actually come, but was grateful she had. Especially considering the news she'd brought.

"You know Callie," Laurel said as moved into the kitchen to sniff at the pot Saffron had simmering on the stove. "Chicken noodle?" she asked with a gigantic smile.

Saffron nodded. She'd felt a little silly, as a renowned chef, inviting her best friend to dinner and then only offering this simple fare, but it had always been Laurel's favorite. Especially when her world was turning to dust the way it was now. Laurel's need for chicken noodle soup was actually one of the reasons Saffron had decided to become a chef. When they were sophomores, Laurel had bombed her PSATs. She had been sure that meant she had no future whatsoever and had spiraled. So Saffron did the only thing she knew she could to help Laurel out of her funk; she went into the kitchen and pulled out her grandma's old recipes, whipping together the best chicken noodle soup in the Golden State, if Saffron did say so herself.

"It smells incredible," Laurel said after sniffing the air around the pot again.

"Tastes better," Saffron said with a smirk. Saffron was a pretty confident woman in all respects, but when it came to her cooking, she could be downright smug. It was something she'd once worked to curb, and then she'd learned all chefs at her level had huge egos when it came to their food. So why was she trying to hide hers? She deserved to be just as satisfied with her talent, didn't she? So now she wore her pride with ease. She wasn't pompous about it, like some, but she also wasn't willing to downplay her ability. If others didn't like her attitude, she'd give them her food. That typically shut them up.

"I can imagine," Laurel said as Saffron joined her at the stove and dished up two big bowls. Saffron then went to the counter where she had a huge loaf of crusty bread cooling and cut off a few slices, putting them on a plate in the middle of the table along with her butter dish.

"So how are you doing? Really," Saffron asked after they'd sat down and Laurel had dug in. Saffron watched her friend eat, but didn't partake with her. Saffron didn't let much get in the way of her and food, but her stomach was in knots with worry over her friends. Laurel's mess was at the forefront of Saffron's mind, but she also knew that Callie would hardly be eating or sleeping until the problems with the lodge were solved. It didn't seem fair that Saffron got to do either comfortably until she helped ease that burden for Callie. But first, she needed to make sure Laurel was coping.

"This is so good," Laurel said as she set down her spoon.

Saffron was grateful Laurel was actually eating. According to Callie, their friend hadn't had an appetite in the last three days, and judging by the way Callie's clothing nearly hung off of Laurel's body, Saffron could guess her friend hadn't been eating very much before that, either. Stress was a nasty companion.

"So-o-o?" Saffron said the word as three syllables, watching her friend dig back into her meal.

"I'm doing okay. Not great, not even good, but okay," Laurel said as she stirred her soup with her spoon. "I'm scared for Bennie. Heck, I'm scared for me. I've told the kids to stay away and that kills me; I hate that I can't see them, but I don't want this to all come crashing down around them as well. Thankfully, this situation with Bennie is too small to make big city news, so they are somewhat sheltered, for now. I know I've lost everything, but the worst part is I can't even be too mad about that. Because what did I do to deserve the life we had?"

Saffron shook her head and had to interject. "You were a full-time wife and mother. Both essential jobs," Saffron pointed out to her friend.

"I was. And I will forever be grateful I was able to grow up and be exactly who I wanted to be," Laurel said, and Saffron remembered the days following the failed PSAT. After crying for nearly three days straight, Laurel finally came to the conclusion that it didn't matter too much anyway because in the end, she wanted to be a wife and mom. She doubted a future husband would care about her PSAT scores. Although Laurel had, a few months later, retaken the PSATs, crushing them along with the SATs the next year. She'd gone to college and graduated in early childhood education with honors. The woman was a genius but tended to sell herself short. She'd point out that Kenzie, Saffron, and Callie all had thriving careers and even Hazel had her interior design Instagram account that was a job in and of itself. And although Saffron agreed that she and her friends had been successful, she hated that Laurel couldn't see all that she had accomplished, not because she was Bennie's wife, but just as Laurel.

"I continued to stay at home even after the kids left for college. I could have looked for a job then, but I chose to stay in my cushy life."

"We all would have. Getting back into the rat race after twenty-plus years away would be terrifying," Saffron pointed out, and Laurel nodded. "And you had no idea your husband was swindling his clients."

Laurel flinched, and Saffron wished she hadn't been so blunt. But she wasn't known to hold back, even when she probably should.

"Sorry," Saffron said with a grimace.

Laurel shook her head. "It's the truth," she responded and then sighed.

"I know. I know all of what you're saying, but it's still hard to live, you know? I put all of my trust in one man; I didn't even question whether anything was up. Ever. I allowed myself to completely rely on him."

"Isn't that marriage? Complete trust?" Saffron asked.

"But I didn't just trust him, I let him carry me through life. When anything went wrong, I dropped the problem in Bennie's lap. I guess I figure this is now my penance. The biggest problem I've ever faced and I have to do it alone," Laurel nearly whispered the last words, her voice full of emotion.

"Have you talked to him?" Saffron asked, and Laurel shook her head.

"Some days I want to. Or think I do. I'm so mad, and I need answers. But then I'll get scared and decide I don't want answers. So I chicken out. He's tried to call me a few times, but nothing like I assumed he would. I've disappeared from his life for three days, and he's called a handful of times. Never leaving a message. I'm sure he knows where I am. Rosebud is too small for secrets, so he knows I'm okay and I guess that's enough. I just...I want him to care more, but I also want to be able to hate him. Now that he's just gone, it feels like I get none of that. And then I'm back in my circle where I think I don't deserve anything I want and...."

Saffron shook her head, trying to give herself a few more moments to compose her thoughts. Laurel had it all wrong. She hadn't done anything to deserve this. She was being shunned by the town, and she was the biggest victim of all.

"This is the bravest I've ever seen you be. The bravest I've ever seen anyone," Saffron said instead of trying to fight Laurel's earlier accusations against herself.

"Brave?" Laurel scoffed.

"I'm serious, Laurel. This situation is one of nightmares. And you walked into that house..."

"With Hazel."

"Who cares who you were with? You did it. *You* faced that. And now you have no idea what your future holds, and yet here you sit, smiling, caring about our friend's problems."

"The lodge is all of our problem."

"See, even that. You're taking ownership. You are looking around and seeing us even when you have every right to shut down and only worry about you."

Laurel shook her head again, and Saffron knew it was going to take more than one conversation for her friend to see the reality that she was smart and brave and loved for herself, but Saffron felt this was enough of a start.

"Speaking of the lodge..." Laurel said as she straightened in her seat.

Saffron knew it was time to move on. She'd said her piece, and Laurel would stew over it. It was Laurel's way. And then, hopefully, Saffron's words would penetrate and Laurel would understand how truly amazing she was.

"Do you think Callie was planning on telling us that she was having issues?" Saffron asked, and Laurel shook her head.

"If she hasn't said anything by now..."

Laurel was right. But didn't Callie see that with five brains they might be able to come up with a plan that Callie's one brain couldn't?

"You keep eating," Saffron said with a wave of her hand toward Laurel. "I'll think."

Laurel didn't have to be told more than once, and she got back to her dinner while Saffron nibbled at a piece of bread.

"So what exactly did Hazel tell you?" Saffron asked.

"The family doesn't want to sell because Sue hates Hazel," Laurel explained between bites of chicken noodle.

"And Hazel just told you this?" Saffron asked, thinking it was unlike Hazel to give up any secrets. And it seemed like Callie had told Hazel about the problems in confidence.

Laurel paused her eating. "Um, I might have overheard something a few days ago when they thought I was sleeping, and then I may have used the pity you all feel for me right now to get some answers from Hazel?" Laurel said, looking about as contrite as a puppy caught with her owner's favorite shoe in her mouth.

Saffron had to laugh. She wasn't upset by Laurel's actions in the least. It seemed that this problem with the lodge was helping her not to mope, which would have been acceptable behavior considering how her life was falling apart, but Saffron liked this side of Laurel. Like all of them, Laurel could be a fighter when she chose to be. And it looked like right now she was deciding to fight. And Saffron would take fighting Laurel over sad Laurel any day of the year.

"I knew I loved you for a reason," Saffron said with a grin.

Laurel pretended to be offended. "You better love me for much more than that. Although, I have to admit, the reason I love you? This soup." Laurel pointed to her bowl with her spoon, and this time it was Saffron who put on an act of feigned offense. They had both loved each other for too long and been through too much to ever doubt that the love they had was true. The love they had for each member of their little group. That love was truer than any other love Saffron had in her life, other than for her family.

"And why does Sue hate Hazel?" Saffron asked, knowing they needed to get back to the task at hand. "Isn't it kind of crazy that she's holding on to a grudge from *high school*?"

"Yeah, I thought the same thing. Especially that the family is letting her continue to hold that grudge? But then again, I'm not sure the family knows why Sue is vetoing us, just that she is. And I'm sure they wouldn't be okay with it if there weren't a big developer in the wings about to come in with what will probably be a much better offer," Laurel explained, and Saffron crossed her arms.

This was a problem. But not one they couldn't solve.

"Why does Sue hate Hazel?"

"Two words. Dylan Pinnegar," Laurel said, and Saffron let out a guffaw.

"Seriously? A boy?"

Laurel nodded.

"Evidently Sue still blames Hazel for running the love of her life out of town," Laurel joked, and Saffron laughed even though this really wasn't a laughing matter. But better to laugh than to cry.

"Did you know I saw Dylan the other day?" Saffron asked.

"He's back in town?" Laurel's eyes went wide.

"Moved back to help take care of his parents, according to him," Saffron said, and Laurel nodded. They were getting to the age where that was happening more and more. "And he can run his tattoo shops from anywhere; his artists do most of the day-to-day work anyway, so he thought why not come home?"

Laurel clapped once. "Can you think of an any more perfect occupation for Dylan? I'm glad he moved beyond his rebel-without-a-cause stage and found himself."

Saffron nodded. "And not only found himself but found himself rich. Does that make sense?" Saffron asked.

Laurel shook her head but then added, "But I get what you meant. Dylan's rich."

Saffron nodded again. "Evidently tattoos are good business."

"Who would have thought?" Laurel shrugged her slight shoulders.

Saffron couldn't help but think that Laurel's life finally exploding might have been good for her. She seemed freer, less like she was holding all of her cares with her everywhere she went. Sure, all of the fallout had to stink for her, but seeing her like this? Saffron hoped this was the beginning of something great for her friend.

"And guess who he asked me about?" Saffron asked, and Laurel's eyes went wide again.

"He still has a thing for Hazel?" Laurel asked, and Saffron nodded.

"Said he read about her divorce on the internet," Saffron replied, and Laurel laughed.

"I'm guessing he might have had a twofold reason for coming home?" Saffron added.

Laurel shook her head. "If any woman could cause a man to carry a torch for her for twenty-plus years and through a marriage, it would be our Hazel."

Saffron had to agree. She couldn't imagine any man pining for her for that long. Heck, she couldn't imagine any man pining for her period.

"But that doesn't help us, does it?" Laurel asked, and Saffron let her mind whirl with possibilities.

"Maybe it could?" Saffron picked up her phone and texted her friends to meet her at Callie's office the next morning.

———

"THIS IS INSANE," Hazel said as she leaned back in her seat, her face set in a defiant stare directed at Saffron.

Other than the dark circles under her eyes, one would never know Hazel was going through her own trying time. She'd told them that she was coming to terms with Chase moving across the country, but Saffron knew it had to be killing her friend. Her children were everything to her. And for Chase to choose his father instead...well, the dark circles were understandable. But Hazel was putting on a brave face, especially for Sterling's sake. And right now, her brave face looked a little scary. Especially because it was pointed at Saffron.

"But it might actually work," Callie said quietly from where she stood in the corner of her office. She'd offered all of the available seats to her friends and opted to stand. She'd been pacing before; she hadn't liked that everyone had been let in on what she felt was her failure, but her pacing had ceased when Saffron had presented her plan.

"Really?" Hazel asked, questioning her earlier negativity but still far from seeming convinced. It was one thing for Saffron to present a crazy plan. It was another for Callie, the queen of logistics, to think it might actually work.

"Not only could Saffron's plan get Sue to forgive you, the

developer has come into a few issues as well," Callie said with a smirk.

The women all turned to her, waiting for an explanation.

"I haven't lived in this town all my life just to be beaten out on an offer by an out-of-towner."

That was not enough of an explanation, at least in Saffron's book.

"So what did you do?" Kenzie asked. Evidently, it wasn't enough for Kenzie either.

"Found a few town statutes and brought them to the attention of the town council. I was so focused on us and how our deal could be worked out that I wasn't even thinking outside of the box in the way I normally do. But after some good sleep and a couple long showers, it came to me. The lodge isn't just important to us, it's a town treasure. That's why we love it. That's why we want it. No one would want to see it torn down, right? Thanks to those statutes I found, the lodge *could* be deemed as historic, according to the town bylaws," Callie said. "Doesn't mean it will be, it would have to be approved by the council, but I think I could convince more than half of them to approve. Most of them have been on my side anytime I want to do something to preserve the town. And if the lodge is deemed a historic building, the developer wouldn't be able to divide up the land into as many lots, not with the lodge that sits right in the middle of all that land. It would surely cost more that it would be worth to the developer to keep the lodge up to town standards if all he really wants is the land. He'd have not only fewer lots, but he'd have to make all kinds of improvements to the actual building he'd rather tear down. We, on the other hand, would make those improvements along with so many more without being forced to."

"Because we want to keep the lodge and the surrounding land just as it is," Laurel said with a nod of understanding.

"With a few upgrades," Saffron added, thinking about the kitchen she'd been promised.

"Right. And this would not only deter this developer, it would deter all developers. Leaving us as the only offer on the table," Callie said with a huge grin.

"So this developer and every future developer loses and we're the only offer. That's all great news," Hazel said. "But nowhere in there do I understand why we have to go through with Saffron's nutty plan."

"Because the town council isn't on my side yet, so I could still fail. The possibility puts pressure on the family, but by no means is it a done deal. If we gave them another offer, with slightly better terms, and Sue wasn't against us..."

"The lodge would be ours," Saffron finished Callie's thought.

"So we wait to see how it plays out. If the town council doesn't vote our way...."

"Do you really want to take that chance, Hazel?" Kenzie interrupted quietly.

"She's right. It is a big chance we're taking if we don't do everything we can right now," Saffron said. "Someone could come in with another offer between now and everything working out with the town council. Historic buildings could bring in a whole new kind of competitor. But if Callie comes in with pressure on the developer, and if Sue finally forgives you, giving the family no reason to say no to us, it would be like an immediate full court press."

Hazel rubbed a hand over her face. "And all I have to do is go on a date with Dylan Pinnegar."

"We need some leverage so that he'll apologize to Sue for leaving town," Saffron stated. "He promised he'd be happy to do so. He feels badly about the way he left things with Sue."

"So why do I have to go on a date with him?" Hazel asked, raising her hands in exasperation.

"Because he's a smart man. He knows this might be his only way to get a date with you," Callie said with a wink.

Hazel huffed.

"I swear he's even better looking than he was in high school." Saffron recalled the man she'd spoken to. His dark hair was now sprinkled with a bit of gray, but the salt-and-pepper look worked for Dylan. His shoulders were broader than they had been, and it looked like he'd allowed his artists to do a bit of work on him. Between all of that and his dark-green eyes that had always made Hazel swoon, she wasn't going to be sorry about going on a date with Dylan Pinnegar.

"I doubt that," Hazel said with a swift shake of her head. "But even if he were, I'm not dating anymore," Hazel said, causing Laurel to laugh.

"Oh, you're serious," Laurel said, chuckles evaporating as she took in Hazel's straight face.

"Yes, I'm serious. I've decided I'm done with men," Hazel stated.

"For how long?" Saffron asked, raising an eyebrow.

"Forever!" Hazel sounded sufficiently frustrated with the male species, but they all knew her too well to believe that she'd really given up on all men.

"Look where men got me." Hazel waved her hand in the air.

"Two beautiful children, a gorgeous home, enough savings that you'll never have to work again," Kenzie deadpanned, and Saffron had to bite her lip to keep from laughing.

Hazel glared at Kenzie and then sighed because she knew she'd lost.

"Fine. One date. Because this is my fault, not because of Dylan and his supposed sizzling hotness," Hazel acquiesced.

Saffron was about to continue teasing her friend because no one had said anything about sizzling hotness, but then she looked at Hazel's stressed face and let it go. Their friend had endured enough of their harassment for one afternoon.

"But do you really think Sue will let go of her grudge after a single apology from Dylan? I tried multiple times, along with offering a private concert from Wells Harrington. She's got a heart of stone," Hazel said.

Saffron shrugged. "Isn't it worth a shot?"

Kenzie was the first to nod, followed by Callie and Laurel. Hazel looked around the office and then finally joined in.

Saffron grinned. She had a feeling this was going to work.

CHAPTER THIRTEEN

"ISN'T Dylan just as attractive as I said he was?" Saffron asked Hazel.

It had been a few days since Hazel had gone out with him, and though she still wouldn't admit it to any of them, Callie could tell she'd had a really good time. And that scared Hazel. So she'd gone to one of her best methods of defense. She was denying, denying, denying.

"He's fine, I guess," Hazel said as she leaned back against the frame of her car.

"Oh, he's *fine* all right," Saffron said with a smirk, and Hazel rolled her eyes.

"Enough about Dylan," Callie said, rescuing Hazel. As much fun as it was to hear about Hazel's love life, this was more important.

Where they stood was exactly where they had all wanted to be for months. Longer even—for Callie, it had been *decades* of waiting. "Now, this is a sight to behold," she said as the five women looked up at their future.

The lodge loomed before them, everything they'd hoped for. And it was theirs now. It had finally come to pass.

"I can't believe Saffron's stupid plan worked," Hazel muttered.

"Saffron's *brilliant* plan was what I think you meant to say," Saffron added, her smirk still firmly in place. She wasn't about to let Hazel live that down anytime soon.

"It's kind of sad that all Sue needed was an apology," Laurel said as she shaded her eyes from the sun so that she could look up at the green roof of the lodge.

"An apology along with some well-placed rumors that got to the rest of the McPhersons, letting them know the town council would soon be voting but that our offer would be gone long before that," Callie said with what her friends liked to call her evil grin. She couldn't help it. When she got her way, she felt a bit evil. In the best way possible.

"Do you think this place needs a new roof?" Laurel asked as she brought her eyes back to ground level.

Callie nodded. That had been revealed during inspection.

"Along with a good power wash," Kenzie stated.

"And it looks like portions of the front porch are rotting," Hazel added, and Callie felt like her friends were getting a little lost in the physical troubles the lodge. She needed them to keep seeing her vision.

"I see it all," Saffron said as she climbed up onto the wooden railing that divided the lodge's land from the surrounding vineyard. "But I can also see five eighteen-year-old girls. Remember them?"

Callie felt her eyes mist up as she nodded. Of course she could see them. Those girls were all she saw any time she looked at this lodge.

"One thought that marrying the swoony and sexy country star would take her on a whirlwind adventure that fulfilled her every dream," Hazel admitted softly, and Callie knew her friend was still hurting from her divorce and, most of all, stinging from the pain of missing her oldest son.

"And another thought that as long as she had enough money, there was no problem that could touch her," Kenzie added even quieter than Hazel had been.

Kenzie wouldn't talk about it, so all Callie knew was that Bryan had moved back to their condo in the city and Kenzie, although she hid it well, was mourning his loss. Callie was pretty sure Kenzie had told them nothing because she knew nothing. He'd left but she hoped with enough time he'd come back. But who knew?

"And the most foolish of all thought that she could place all of her everything with one man. She never even considered what life would look like if that man failed her," Laurel said, her voice sounding loud compared to the whispers of her friends. Saffron climbed down from the fence and stood next to Laurel, offering her support if she needed or wanted it.

"But as foolish as she was, I think she'd be proud of all of us now. Even though it took her thirty-some years, that girl is finally doing something with her life. Something she wants to do. Something she needs to do," Laurel continued as she linked arms with Kenzie and Saffron who were on either side of her. Saffron took Hazel's arm, who then slipped her arm through Callie's, connecting them all.

"I'm pretty proud of us too," Callie said as she leaned her head on Hazel's arm.

"Will you still be proud of us when you find out I've never held a paintbrush in my life?" Kenzie said, and the women began to laugh.

"Don't worry. I'll teach you, Kenz," Hazel promised.

And that was when Callie knew they would all be just fine. They were each hurting or dealing with their own issues. Saffron's business partners were drawing out proceedings in a way that Saffron's lawyer said made it feel like a divorce instead of a simple business dissolution. And Callie still felt an emptiness in her heart and life, although with her friends around, she had to admit that hole felt a bit smaller.

But when all was said and done, they each had the others in their little group. When Kenzie failed in painting, Hazel would lift her. When Callie failed at solving their problems, Saffron would come in with her off-the-wall solutions. And when Laurel needed a place to land, they'd all catch her. It was what they'd been doing since high school, and it was what they would always do. It was why this lodge would soon again be the shining jewel it once had been. Callie began to imagine the place full and bustling, Rosebud's entire economy thriving.

They could do this. They *would* do it.

Together.

Made in the USA
Middletown, DE
15 July 2022

69399192R00096